Carnal Voices

An African American Erotica Collection of Short Stories

V.T. Green

ISBN-13: 9798479306204
ISBN-10: 1477123456

Cover design by: Art Painter
Library of Congress Control Number: 2018675309
Printed in the United States of America

Contents

Hard Choices

"This bout the be the last time I make this trip. Swear, she ain't even that fine for me to be wasting my fucking gas!" Jaren speaks to no one in particular. No one else occupies the car, just Jaren and his thoughts. The frown covering his face reveals he's second-guessing his decision. He attempts to understand why he's driving 40 minutes to see a woman he cares nothing for. The tension on his face relaxes when he recalls how well she takes the dick. He speaks aloud frustratedly, "I don't even care for her like that, but here I am, *again*, driving 30 miles out my way on a Friday night for some pussy. Barely had gas to get to work this week, now I'm fucking off my paycheck already! This some simp shit." Jaren shakes his head.

"Damn!" Jaren slams on his brakes. The traffic light changes red as he approaches the intersection. Jaren slows to a complete stop, allowing his thoughts to run rampant in hopes to settle on a decision whether he should make the drive or not. He says aloud, "I know should turn around before I get on this freeway."

He checks his phone while waiting for the light to change. A text from Zadora, sent two minutes ago, displays in the notification panel.

The door is open

"Fuck! J, this the last time she taste this dick. For real, for real." He throws his phone on the passenger seat out of frustration. The traffic light changes green. Jaren speeds off, his turn signal signifies his choice when he merges onto the interstate.

∞ ∞ ∞

Jaren parks in front of the old red brick house. He checks himself out in the rearview mirror and presses the power button on his phone before exiting the car. The less distractions the better, as he plans to get in and get out. Jaren approaches the door, cautiously turning the knob and peeking inside. The house is dimly lit and smells like she recently cooked chicken or something. He steps inside, closing the door behind him.

He takes a few more steps into the living room. "ZZ, where you at?"

ZZ appears from the hallway to greet Jaren. The short cut-off shorts and purple crop top on her petite frame cause him to shift in his stance. She extends her arms for a hug. He wraps her in his arms and leans down to kiss her. Zadora questions his lack of communication over the past couple of months. "How you been? Haven't heard from you in a while. Was surprised when you called."

Jaren's gaze wanders over her body. "Yeah, been busy. My girl been acting funny." He pauses. "I missed you," he says, placing another kiss on her lips. Jaren insists she didn't detect his lies. He has no girlfriend, nor has he missed her. Why did he lie to a woman not pressing him for time or a commitment?

She rolls her eyes at his obvious lies. He's predictable, calling only on Thursdays to come over on Friday. Unnecessarily and habitually lying about everything and nothing. ZZ knows he doesn't have a girlfriend because he fucks way too long and cums too much to have a steady girlfriend. If his dick wasn't so big, she could have easily cut him off months ago. But even with that big dick, he may never keep a woman if he doesn't learn to fuck. Second, he's broke and not trying to fix it.

"You hungry?" ZZ asks Jaren, "I made baked chicken and rice." She really cooked for her friend Tony, but he hasn't hit her back yet.

"Not right now. Maybe later." Jaren takes a seat on the blue suede sofa. "Come over here." He motions for ZZ to sit with him. Instead of allowing her to sit, he pulls her down into his lap, kissing her hungrily. His hands roam her body, easing under her shirt to fondle her perky breasts. Just like always, his sex game is stale and one-dimensional.

ZZ straddles his lap and grinds her hips against his growing erection. "Hold on a sec," she stands from his lap and exits the living room, returning with yellow fabric rope. This may be a good opportunity to for her to try a few sex toys before taking him out of rotation. She pulls a chair from the small round wooden dining table. "Come here and sit down." She motions by curling her index finger back and forth. She waits with her hands on her hips for Jaren to respond.

"What the fuck?" Jaren remains in his seat, attempting to stall while he thinks of something clever to say. "Tell me why first. What you trying to do, Z?" He shakes his head in disbelief of the situation unfolding. He's never trusted a girl to take it to this level of kinkiness. Jaren recalls the freakiest sex he's experienced. He once met a Haitian girl at a Miami bar on a trip with his boys. He invited her back to his room. While fucking she unexpectedly asked him to choke her while he came on her face. Not knowing he would love it as much as he did, of course, he tried the exact same move on another girl, but it didn't go as expected. She hit him, cursed him out, and ghosted his texts.

Jaren rises from his seat, curiosity getting the best of him. "For real, what you trying to do?" He gives an intimidating stare. ZZ maintains her stance, staring back in his eyes, growing impatient. He breaks the eye contact and reluctantly sits in the chair.

ZZ circles around the chair. Her voice in a low, seductive tone. "Why you gotta be so stubborn? All I'm gonna do is tie you to the chair so I can have my way with you. That's why you came here right?" After months of the same routine, though never discussed, they consciously agreed the relationship is strictly physical.

Shivers creep through Jaren's body as he imagines her doing freaky things to him. "Yeah, you always get me right. You ain't never went this far though."

ZZ tugs his shirt, signaling him to raise his arms. She removes his shirt. Her hands rub over his tattoo-covered chest. His thick, solid body makes him nearly twice her size.

ZZ uses the rope to amateurly tie Jaren's hands behind the chair like he's getting arrested. "Is that too tight?" She tugs on the knot to make sure it's secure.

"Yeah, I guess."

"Good." ZZ returns to face Jaren. Kneeling in front of him, her hands caress up and down his thighs. The slow and melodic movements release tension from his body. She unbuckles his belt, then unbuttons and unzips his jeans. ZZ slides her right hand down his pants to release his growing erection from bondage. He lifts his lower body, allowing ZZ to pull his pants down to his ankles.

ZZ stands, exiting the living area again. Jaren yells, "Yo, come on! This ain't cool, bro!" He drops his head knowing he's losing control of the situation fast. Jaren looks up to find ZZ has returned with more rope. His eyebrows lift with suspicion.

ZZ asks, "I'm giving you a choice. Either you get blindfolded, or I bind your legs. Which one?"

Jaren's head tilts slightly. He heard her loud and clear. 'What type of choice is that?' he thinks to himself. "Z, we ain't never got down like this. What's this about?" He contemplates how far this will go. He's both curious and nervous. Not to mention concerned if she'd tell anybody about what they do.

"Answer me or I'll choose for you!" She knows he wants it, whatever 'it' is. ZZ's sexual experience proves most men are freaks but act aloof in the moment.

After no response from Jaren, ZZ decides to make a move of her own. She removes her crop top t-shirt over her head. Jaren's eyes widen at the sight of her small bare breasts near his face. ZZ positions herself to stand directly between Jaren's knees. He leans in, opening his mouth to suck one of her nipples. Her mouth parts, releasing a pleasurable sigh. He flicks his tongue and pinches her hardened nipple with his lips. Jaren flicks his tongue against her hardened nipple. ZZ feels her juices flow out of her vagina. Slowly, she steps back, removing her nipple from his warm mouth. ZZ covers his eyes with a blue silk scarf, tying a small knot to secure it in place.

Jaren is quiet. He's usually talkative. The huge smile on his face and his hard erection are evidence of his enjoyment. "You should have answered me, Jaren. Now I get to have my way with you." She playfully smushes his face.

ZZ kneels in front of Jaren, staring intently at the big, hard dick in front of her. Her small, delicate hands barely cover the base, leaving inches and the tip uncovered. She licks her lips and lowers her mouth around the head of his dick. Jaren moans from anticipation. ZZ removes her hand, allowing her big lips to swallow him deep into her mouth, leading to him adjusting in his seat.

She comes up for air only to grab the remaining rope from the table. Her hands easing down his thighs, ZZ uses the remaining rope to secure his ankles to the chair's legs.

In a low tone, Jaren asks, "Damn, you showing out. Got me all tied up and shit. What you about to do?"

Standing to enter the kitchen nearby, she opens the cabinet and retrieves a glass. She places the glass under the refrigerator's automatic ice maker, filling it with crushed ice.

Jaren grows agitated by his vulnerable state. "You really making something to drink right now? What the fuck! Got my dick all out!" He tries to move, but his body is completely bound to the chair. ZZ smiles witnessing him struggle to break free.

"Jaren, you always talking shit when you come over here. Like you 'Mr. Put it Down' or something. Negro, please!" ZZ says sarcastically.

"Stop playing, Zadora. For real. Come untie me." He lowers his voice knowing it'd be horrifying if she flipped out crazy. ZZ has never acted aggressively toward him, but her actions today prove he doesn't know her as well as he thought. "What's up with you?"

ZZ rolls her eyes for the second time tonight as she returns to the dining area. "Don't talk so much."

She removes a few pieces of crushed ice from the glass, placing them into her mouth allowing them to melt against her warm tongue. Repeatedly, she takes more ice into her mouth, kneels between his legs again, and takes him into her mouth. His body jolts from the coldness of the ice. "Oh shit!"

Her head slowly bobs up and down his dick. Jaren growls and grows harder with each stroke. ZZ lowers her head, taking him deeper into her mouth, swallowing more than her mouth can fit. She heaves on his dick, but doesn't stop. She goes for it again, and again, and again. Not giving up easily, ZZ takes him deep into her throat, her nose runs and her attempt to deepthroat him is still unsuccessful. ZZ slurps the saliva running down his dick before speaking. "Do you want to come in my mouth or my ass?"

"Huh?" Jaren's mind was in a trance listening to her suck his dick. He's slightly annoyed because she's real close to fucking his nut up. "What you say?"

She repeats herself: "You want to cum in my mouth or my ass?"

Jaren thinks before responding. He's confident he can go a second round for the pussy. Getting head seems like the favorable choice.

"Answer me."

ZZ stands. Jaren hears her footsteps trailing off down the hallway. He yells out, "Your mouth."

Jaren mumbles under his breath. "If she leave me here one more time..." With no idea of what he will actually do if she does leave him there again, he keeps convincing himself he's still in control. Her returning footsteps thump hard against the hardwood floors. She returns to the dining area with a small box and a bottle of lubricant. She opens the box revealing a small vibrating butt plug. The rumbling of plastic prompts Jaren to ask what's going on. "What's that?"

ZZ assumes, since they've already gone this far, she might as well make the effort worth it.

"It's a gift! You want it?" ZZ stares intently to read his facial expressions. Even though she can't see his eyes, the lines in his forehead and flared nostrils tell her he's frustrated. Shockingly, Jaren nods his head yes.

Melting more ice in her mouth before kneeling, she sticks out her tongue. Slowly licking up the shaft of his dick, she sucks the head into her mouth. The sound resembles that of a champagne cork when she releases the head from her lips. The pop echoes through the room. His dick twitches.

ZZ picks up the bottle of lubrication and squeezes a small amount in her hand. She coats the butt plug with a generous amount and lowers her upper body to take his balls into her mouth.

"Hmm," a moan escapes Jaren's lips. Her big, wide mouth offers more room to gently flick her tongue against his balls. ZZ uses her free hand to play with his gooch, rubbing it gently. He shifts his body down in the chair so she can access it easier. ZZ bites his inner thigh, testing his pain tolerance. Jaren growls but doesn't contest her advances. He wants more. He wants her to take whatever she wants.

"You like it?" she asks.

Jaren doesn't respond, but his body does. She feels his muscles slowly relax into her hands and his breaths getting deeper. ZZ proceeds by gripping his thigh, spreading his legs wider, and licking his balls again. She lightly rubs the vibrating butt plug against his gooch, slowly inching closer to his asshole. ZZ then strokes his dick with one hand while slowly inserting the butt plug with the other. Jaren's mouth parts and his breathing is labored.

She didn't expect it would be that easy. His appearance resembles a dope boy from the toughest hood. She knows he's a good guy underneath his armor, but he fucks her the same way every time. He eats the pussy, slangs dick, and fucks hard. He's left her unsatisfied one too many times.

She holds the butt plug in place with light pressure and proceeds with sucking his dick again. With her mouth around the head, she works her hand up his shaft. ZZ jerks him off. She takes him deep into her mouth. The head touches the back of her throat, and she lets saliva fall from her mouth down to his balls.

"Fuck, Z!" says Jaren in a husky tone.

Jaren is on the edge. He listens intensely to her gag on his dick, nearly throwing up in his lap. She strokes his dick, slurping the head, and picking up speed when he hardens in her hand. Jaren's dick begins to throb against her hand. "Oh shit!" Jaren exclaims as his body tenses. He inhales a hefty breath of air. He can't tap her shoulder because his hands are tied, so he calls out, "Z!"

A few strokes later he releases hard, heaving uncontrollably. She moans after swallowing his cum, humming in a low tone on his dick. Pleased with her work, she removes his softened dick from her mouth, looking up to find Jaren's chin resting against his chest. He is exhausted yet thoroughly satisfied. He smiles at the story he'll one day get to tell about this experience.

ZZ debates if she wants to wait for the dick or call her fuck buddy, Tony. She unties his ankles from the chair. Silence lingers in the air. She stands and circles around him, stopping to untie his hands and remove the blindfold.

"You liked that shit. Don't lie and say you didn't."

A sly smile covers his face. "Yeah, I wasn't expecting all that."

ZZ walks toward the kitchen and places the rope on the counter. "So, what you about to do?" she asks.

A look of shock or possible hurt shows on Jaren's face. He knows what the line means all too well. He's used it plenty of times before. "Umm, I was about to eat some of that chicken you cooked and give you round two. But sound like you on some other shit." He grabs his pants settled around his ankles, stands and pulls up his pants.

"No, not that. Me and my girls going out tonight and I need to get ready," she blatantly lies.

He gathers his shirt off the floor. "Y'all coming to the city? You want to hit me when you done?"

The frown on ZZ's face is full disdain for his comments. "Let's not do this. You don't like me like that. You only come over to fuck. I get it, but don't pretend right now."

Jaren responds, "It's not like that. I thought that's what you wanted." He doesn't even believe his own lies. Maybe he would have taken her more seriously if he had known she was this type of freak. He struggles to find the words to salvage the relationship. "Zadora, don't be like that. I chose to come see you because I like you."

"No, you chose to come see me cause you wanted pussy. You chose head and that's what you got. She pauses briefly. "Hey, I really need to get ready. Maybe we'll talk later sometime," ZZ says walking towards the door. She wastes no time guiding him out of her house and out of her life.

"Don't be like that though. Come on." Jaren follows her and wraps his arms around her. He likes her, but don't *like her* like her. That doesn't mean he expected she would rid him out of her life. This was not what Jaren was expecting tonight. He knows she'll come back around.

"I'm gonna hit you up." He steps in closer, placing a peck on her lips, "Okay?"

ZZ doesn't respond. They stand in silence.

Jaren smiles and exits the front door. ZZ watches his shadowy figure disappear down the driveway. She closes the door, and leans her back against it. "Hold up! That negro still got that damn butt plug in!

She giggles to herself, "I did say it was a gift, huh?"

Game Day

Giovanni enters the kitchen from the outdoor deck. I yell, "Thought you were going to help me cook today! First off, you wouldn't go the grocery store, then you barely helped me clean up earlier!" His long hair is pulled back in a ponytail. He wears a gray faded Miami Dolphins t-shirt. Out of habit, I glimpse down at the dick print showing in his red basketball shorts. If he didn't already piss me off today, I would take the dick right here in the kitchen. "Gio!"

He's distracted by whatever's on his phone. "Huh?"

"I said why you not helping? This your party!"

We met on a dating site three years ago. After a couple of weeks of phone calls and messaging, we set-up a dinner date. Yeah, sure we fucked the first night. It was more than incredible, and guess what? He hasn't left me alone since. Six months into our relationship, he moved from Miami to my townhouse in Fort Lauderdale. Giovanni is half Italian, named after a great uncle. His mother is black American and his father is Italian. He's handsome, but his ugly ways are growing more and more irritating.

Gio drops an empty aluminum pan on the counter. "What? I am helping. I just put the meat on the grill. See?" he says with a playful smile. He stands all up in my personal space. I roll my eyes at his humorless joke. "Monika, baby, don't act like that." His body irritatingly presses against my side. He towers over me, standing at an entire foot taller than my 5'4" frame.

Last minute, he decides to throw a barbeque. Well, it's last minute to me. Today is Saturday, and he didn't mention his plans until Thursday night. He springs this on me and expected me too just be cool with it. This is what happened.

Gio dropped off my car at the dealership to fix a sensor light. He was supposed to pick me up from work. When I got off, he wouldn't answer his phone. I waited for over an hour before calling a ride share to pick me up. By the time I got home, he was sitting on the couch playing his video game. I went the fuck off! The argument was bad bad. After make-up sex later that night, he had the nerve to sneak in a mention of the party.

No lie. The sex is still amazing, but I know I should've left him a long time ago. He hasn't done anything for me in months. No dates, no trips, no flowers. Just sex. The arguments are becoming more frequent since his promotion to sales director at a local Lexus dealership. I understand his job is important, but that's no excuse. He finds time for everything and everybody, but me.

All he ever does is work, watch sports, play video games, and party every weekend. He goes out to a club or bar nearly every Saturday night. Not to mention, he can't do nothing for himself. No cleaning, laundry, grocery shopping, nothing. Plus, he barely contributes financially. It's a hassle to get him to help with the bills. To say I am tired of taking care of his grown ass is an understatement.

Attempting to prepare the house for guests, I've been cleaning and cooking since early morning. I promised myself I wasn't going to fuck up his day, especially since some of his friends are visiting from out of state. "Can you at least turn off the potatoes on the stove?" I ask. It's almost three o'clock in the afternoon. His friends are due to arrive around five to watch their alma mater, University of Miami, play tonight.

This is not how I planned to spend my Saturday. We could have taken a boat trip to the Caribbean or flew to Atlanta. Anything but this.

Gio leans against the kitchen island, "What all you cooking baby?"

How can he act so clueless? He sent a long ass text message of what he wanted on the menu. Filled with frustration, I reply,

"I'm making everything you asked. Burgers, chicken, potato salad, mac n' cheese, baked beans, right? Did I miss something?"

He hugs me from behind, placing light kisses on my cheek. His mustache pricking my face. "Yep. You not on the menu?" he says. Gio must have sensed my irritation because he backs away and quietly exits the patio door.

"Trifling ass," I say under my breath.

Game Day - Ch. 2

The doorbell rings. Gio exits the bar area to answer the door. He's showered, dressed, and everything else. All the while, I'm still cooking and looking like a disheveled hot mess.

"You made it bro!" Gio says.

"Yooo, what's good G? How you been bro?" his friend, Justin, says. They went to college together, but Justin moved to Chicago for a job a few years back. He looks more mature now since growing a goatee. He looks well with his glowing brown skin and short-cropped, freshly cut curly hair. Gio didn't mention Justin, specifically, was coming to town. This must be the reason he intended on planning the weekend. The omission is highly unusual, with Justin being is his closest friend.

Justin walks over to greet me. "Hey Mona. How you been?" Justin is the only person who calls me Mona. I asked him about it once. He mentioned something off the wall about the Mona Lisa. I was too buzzed to care. It never bothered me, so I let it ride.

"Hey Justin. I've been okay. How's everything in Chicago?" I really wish I had time to get dressed before people started showing up. Luckily, I only need to start the dishwasher and place the baked beans in the oven.

Justin gives me a friendly hug. "Just working. Still at the firm. You know me and Natalie broke up a while ago, so I just been enjoying the single life."

"Sorry to hear that, I guess. Y'all were really good together from what I could tell." I say while pouring a glass of white wine.

Gio walks over to the bar and calls out, "J, what you drinking?"

Justin diverts his attention from me and follows Gio to the bar. "What you got over here?" He observes the insane amount of alcohol at the fully stocked bar. It's funny how Gio found time to shop for alcohol last night. "Damn, how many people you expecting? You bought up the whole store. It's about to be one of those nights?" Justin asks with lifted eyebrows.

Gio walks to the fridge and fills the ice bucket. "Man, it's been a while since everybody's been in town at the same time. Thought we could turn up like old times. You did Uber here, right?" Gio laughs.

Picking up my glass of wine, I say, "Gio, I'm heading up upstairs to get dressed." I leave them to their manly bonding or whatever it's called.

In the bedroom, I remove my clothes and place them in the hamper. I enter the bathroom and turn on the shower. Dreading entertaining him and his friends tonight, I take my time showering.

After enjoying the relaxing hot shower and applying some body oil, I slip on a red thong. I enter the closet to rumble through the hangers for decent clothes to wear.

I faintly hear Gio's voice coming closer. "And this our bedroom. Baby, where you at?" He appears in the doorway of the closet with Justin behind him. They both stare at my large D-cup breasts for what seems like minutes.

I shoo him with my hand. "Gio, really? You get on my fucking nerves. Stop staring and go. Damn, get out!"

"My bad, baby. I was just giving Justin a tour." He turns around and pushes Justin. Seconds later, I hear the bedroom door close. There was no reason to bring Justin upstairs. Gio is such a freak, and I wouldn't be surprised if he did that on purpose. Never mind the cute sundress and sandals I planned to wear. Filled with irritation, I dress in a pair of jeans and a red tank top, roughly tying my long braids into a high bun before heading downstairs.

Once I land at the bottom of the stairs, their eyes follow me across the living room to the kitchen. If the music wasn't so insanely loud, you could probably hear their thoughts. Men, I swear!

Gio walks over to me. "Baby, I'm sorry about that. I didn't know you would be umm . . . you, okay?" he says.

"You could have—" Without warning, two men barge through the front door. They didn't knock or ring the doorbell. Maybe they did, but the music drowned it out. Neither of them looks familiar, nor have I seen any pictures of them before.

"Aye, what's up y'all?" the bigger guy says with his arms open wide.

"Bo, come on in my man. Brian, how you been bro?" Gio says, bro-hugging the two guys.

He guides them toward the kitchen. "Baby, this Bolton. We call him Big Bo and this is Brian. We played football together. Y'all this my girl Monika." Big Bo is a dark-skinned big guy with big muscles and long dreads. The other guy, Brian, is shorter, with a lighter complexion, a bald head, full beard, and his arms covered with tattoos.

Politely smiling I say, "Hello. Nice to meet you both."

Brian says, "Nice to meet you Ms. Monika. The food smells good." Why is he flirting? Did anyone else pick up on it? He's cute in a generic kind of way, but it's clear he has plenty of ego.

Gio takes the case of beer from Big Bo's hands and places it in the cooler outside. His friends follow him out onto the deck. Good thing the game will start soon. I plan to retreat to the bedroom for some quiet time, maybe a nap, during the game.

I pry open the patio door off the kitchen. "Gio, can you take the chicken off the grill?"

"Anything for you baby." I hand him an empty pan. Rolling my eyes, I close the door and head back to the stove. I open the oven door to remove the baked beans. When I turn to place them on the counter, a tall, handsome man is standing near the island. I nearly drop the pan to the floor. "You scared me," I say, trying to calm my nerves. "Are you here to watch the game?"

"Yes ma'am! Justin invited me. Sorry to scare you. I knocked a few times before you know. Sorry about that. How you doing?" he rambles. He has an awkward beauty. It could be the eyeglasses and the button up shirt with a front pocket. He has dark wavy hair, walnut brown skin, a slim body resembling a swimmer, and a nice bulge poking in his fitted jeans.

"I'm okay now." I smirk at him. "I'm Monika, Gio's girlfriend. What's your name?"

"LaDarren Hood. Everyone calls me Hood though. It's a military thing," he responds with a smile.

Stirring the baked beans, I look up at him. "You still serve?"

"Yes ma'am, I'm stationed here in Florida right now."

"Well, it's nice to meet you Hood. They're all outside." I point to the patio door. "You can take that door to join them."

"Thank you, Monika," he replies before exiting the door. They erupt in laughter when the door opens. Damn, they are so loud. A long night waits for sure. I line up the pans of food, paper plates, silverware, and napkins on the kitchen island.

Game time is nearing. Gio, Justin, Big Bo, Brian, and Hood return to the living room from the patio. Gio places the pan on the counter, quickly trotting to the living room to turn off the music and turn up the television volume. They are talking loudly and placing bets. I signal to Gio the food is ready. He stands up from his reclining chair and walks toward me.

"The food is ready," I tell him.

"Thank you, baby. I'll tell them."

"Y'all good? I'm about to go upstairs."

He looks around the kitchen. He's already tipsy. His cheeks are blush pink. His smile is big and wide, "We should be good."

Game Day - Ch. 3

It's nearly eight o'clock in the evening when I awake. I stretch and make my way to the bathroom. Feeling refreshed, I head downstairs to check on my house. Gio's eye contact is direct. I become concerned by the serious look on his face. I walk over to him. "What's up?" I ask.

He's loud and drunk. He reaches for my leg to pull me closer. "Hey baby. We up by fourteen right now. Only like four minutes left I think," he slurs his words. I shrug my shoulders letting him know his words don't make sense to me.

Big Bo says, "Yo Monika, that food was hitting! I ate like two plates."

Everybody else chimes in, "So good."

"Fire!"

"Can I take a plate to go?"

I glance at the kitchen to see what mess they left for me to clean. Unenthused, I say, "Please take some. Glad y'all liked it."

Justin asks, "Mona you wanna take a shot? Come on have some fun with us."

"Nope. Justin, don't pull me into this. Somebody gotta be sober," I laugh.

They all begin booing and egging me on. I give in, but only for them to quiet down. I think to myself, 'Why am I doing this?' Probably not the best idea, knowing my tolerance is low. Guess it's a good thing I'm already home. "Okay, okay! Just one though."

Justin picks up the near-empty bottle of tequila from the coffee table. Brian hands him a disposable shot cup, "Here you go."

Gio's drunk ass encourages me, "Go ahead baby!"

The tequila goes down harsh. I consider whether I should have just stayed asleep. I didn't plan on playing with him and his friends.

"Yeeaahh, that's what's up!" Brian says, clapping his hands.

Hood says, "We should play a drinking game. You know how we used to do in college."

"Man, we did so much in college. Which one you talking about, Hood?" Gio asks.

"Shit, it don't matter. We can do 'Guess what'? Y'all remember that one?" Hood says with a smile.

Leaving them be, I walk to the kitchen, refusing to get involved with their games.

The room grows louder. They are laughing and talking at the same time, reminiscing on their college days. Big Bo stands up from the couch, "Shit, wish I could stay and kick it with y'all. Already told my girl I was on my way 20 minutes ago." He makes his rounds bro-hugging and shaking hands with everyone. "It's good seeing y'all though man, for real. We gotta do this again." He stops in front of Brian, "B, you riding out with me or you chilling?"

Brian looks over at Gio and Justin. Gio says, "Up to you. You good if you want to stay."

Brian nods his head, "Alright, I'll chill for a little bit."

At some point after Big Bo left, they turn down the volume of the game on the television and increase the music instead. I was too busy tackling the mess in the kitchen to notice. While putting away the food, I observe them from afar. Whatever game Brian, Justin, and Hood are playing looks similar to rock, paper, scissors. Gio sits there faded, barely hanging with the crowd. I can't discern what's being said. I mind my business and turn my attention back in the direction of the stove and Tupperware.

Lost in my thoughts, I didn't hear anyone approaching. A hard body presses against my back and startles me. Instantly, I turn around to find Hood standing there. "Excuse you? Did you need something?" I ask. He has some nerve. That nerdy look didn't fool me at all.

He replies, "Yes. I didn't get to taste everything." His tone low and deep. He's bold as shit. My mind is overtaken by image of the bulge I witnessed earlier. I look over his shoulder in the direction of the living room. None of the guys are paying us any attention. Gio, Justin, and Brian are quietly staring at the muted TV. Drunk people are not quiet. What kind of game are these dudes trying to play?

It finally occurs to me. How did I not suspect Gio was up to something? In all the three years we dated, he has never invited friends over. We had a conversation a few months ago about threesomes after watching a movie on Netflix. All of a sudden, he insists on throwing an impromptu 'get-together'? This negro think he slick.

I play dumb by rattling off questions. "What do you want, Hood? Why are you so close to me?"

He respectfully steps back, offering space between us. Hood leans in with his voice in a whisper. "I told you what I wanted." He pauses. "You! Let me taste you. Sneak off with me." The perplexed look covering my face may have spooked him. Hood's eyes search mine. It's obvious he's unsure if the game he's playing is worth it. Rejection can turn even the hardest person to mush.

I give direct eye contact, "No, I'm not sneaking off with you. Did you even think to ask what I want?" Clearly, he does not know me. I don't play games and surely don't play fair.

The look on his face is of shock and excitement. "What do you want?" he asks.

"First, I want you to help me clean up this kitchen," I giggle.

He skims over the kitchen with a confused look on his face. "Oh. I umm. Okay, I can do that."

He probably thinks he'll get what he wants by helping me, but I have other plans. I sit at the dining table next to the kitchen. Hood gives me a sexy stare down before scooping macaroni into a Tupperware container.

They are such bad actors. Gio, Justin, and Brian are acting intrigued by whatever is on the TV screen. "Justin!" I yell over the music. Well, that got their attention. They all look my way at the same time, but I only wave Justin to come over. I feel Hood side-eyeing me from the kitchen.

Justin peels himself off the couch and stands in front of me with his back to the living room. "Hey, what's up? You, okay?" He glares at Hood with the look of an angry drunk ready to fight.

I hear the music volume decreasing, so I soften my approach. "Yea, just needed your help with something."

His face show signs of concern. "You know I got you Mona. What you need?"

It may be best if I shoot it straight, wasting no time for him to decipher what I want. "I want you to slowly take off my shirt. Then my pants. Can you do that?" I say in a soft voice for his ears only.

A huge smile spreads across his face. He bites his bottom lip. "Umm, you serious?"

Justin steps closer to me. I nod 'yes.' He motions for me to hold my arms up. I lift my arms, allowing him to raise my shirt up and over my head. He stares for a long moment. Then, he bends down on his knees to unbutton my jeans. His hands shake nervously. Justin locks his eyes with mine as he unzips my jeans. The look in his eyes tells me he has waited for this moment. How long, I'm not sure. It didn't occur to me he was interested until he visited Gio soon after moving to Chicago. We all met for dinner one night, and he couldn't keep his eyes off me.

Well, he now has his moment. I lift my hips to help him tug my tight jeans off my hips. He pulls off my pants and places my right leg over his shoulder, lowering his face between my legs. He nibbles on my pussy through the panties. "Good boy," I say.

I glance quickly over Justin's head into the living room to see Gio and Brian intently watching the show. I then divert my attention to Hood; he begins nervously wiping the counter.

Justin moves my thong to the side and dives in. He slowly laps me up, covering my pussy with his mouth. Loud moans escape my lips. With no objections from Gio by now, I get comfortable.

My suspicions of him setting up this night is proving true.

I place my other leg over Justin's shoulder and scoot down in the chair. Justin's tongue teases my clit with a slow but hard rhythm. Damn it feels good. My moans are growing more frequent. Maybe it's knowing other people are watching. Or maybe he's just damn good at eating pussy. He's incredibly focused. He pace is steady and patient. The pleasurable sensations to my clit intensify quickly. I grab the back of his head and grind his face, rolling my clit against his tongue. I hear him moan with a mouthful and damn near lose it. His tongue feels too good to hold my orgasm in any longer; the release evades me. My body bucks. My thighs squeeze his head until he taps out.

"Thank you," I whimper. Justin gazes at me while kissing my thigh. I remove my legs from his shoulders and immediately check for Hood. He's sitting at the kitchen island. Those glasses hide nothing. The lustful look in his eyes is strong. I scan the kitchen. The containers are on the stove, and the counters are shining. Damn, I could get used to this!

My legs shake as I stand. I insist Justin have my seat. I approach Hood and crowd his personal space. The same as he did to me earlier. He's angled sideways at the counter, giving Gio and Brian a side view of Hood and me. On the other hand, Justin has an up-close view of my ass.

"Do you want to guess what I want now?"

Hood inhales and exhales a long breath. He whispers, "No, tell me."

"I want you to take off your shirt."

Hood pauses briefly, looking me intensely in the eyes. He teasingly unbuttons his shirt. I look down to observe the beautiful body I knew was hiding underneath. I rub my hands over his chest. I begin to unfasten his belt and unbutton his jeans. "Show me your dick, Hood."

The tequila clearly lowered both of our inhibitions. Hood unzips his pants and pulls out his fully erect dick. It's around five inches in length and extremely thick. Without hesitation, I bend down and place the head of his dick against my lips. I tease the tip with light pressure between my lips before opening wide to take it into my mouth. I slowly bob my head up and down, taking in slightly more each time. The girth painfully stretches the corners of my mouth. I imagine I'm riding him. Every stroke I lightly squeeze his dick mimicking my pussy walls contracting around his thick dick. I don't want it to end, but he's losing control by the way he's fucking my face wildly.

He moans deeply. I stop to say, "I want you to cum." Pausing briefly for the words to sink in, then returning to the task at hand. Literally. I take him deeper into my mouth, wetting his dick with the saliva dripping off my tongue. I grind his dick with one hand and cover the tip with my mouth. His hips lift higher with each stroke, and I feel him grow harder in my hand. The pace gradually picks up. Hood is thoroughly enjoying himself, and I follow the rhythm of his body. The wet noises from my mouth echo through the room. "Oh shit," he says and cums in my mouth.

I don't swallow. I open my mouth and let his cum run down my hand into his lap. I remove him from my mouth and lick my lips.

Hood pants with his mouth open, attempting to catch his breath. I leave him there to wash my hands at the kitchen sink. I didn't expect him to release that fast. Thinking to myself, I ask, what now? I feel like an assassin; I could take them all out one by one if I wanted. But this is not one of those nights. I dry my hands and observe the room. Justin is holding his crotch over his jeans. Hood is trying to gather himself. Let me end this little game—time to handle the real issue at hand.

Gio is quietly watching me watch him. In my bra and thong, I strut into the living room. As I pass Brian, he grabs my hand and pulls me into his lap. The sudden movement scares me. "Come here baby girl. What you got for me?" The alcohol lingers on his breath. This is exactly why he was not included in my plans. His aggression was evident when he walked in. Disrespectful from the start. His ego wouldn't allow him to do or say anything I ask of him. Especially with other men in the room. He's the definition of an alpha dickhead.

"Brian, if I wanted to sit on your lap I would have." I attempt to rise from his lap, but he grips my waist. I try again. This time I hear Gio and Justin tell him to ease up. "It's like that?" he questions.

Standing up, I say, "Yes, like that." Then, I turn to Gio, "Can I see you upstairs?"

Gio rises, staggering from his chair. At the top of the stair landing, I turn around to face him. "You know, this hasn't been working for a long while. We always arguing, and you haven't helped me in this relationship since we first started dating. This ain't working for me no more."

"What you talking about? You for real right now?" He says, staggering and scratching his head. "I mean damn baby. Is it because of what happened tonight? I thought you like being pleased. We always be on some freaky shit. I thought you liked it." Turning on my heels, I shake my head. He doesn't get it. In the bedroom, I enter the closet and return with his things. I packed his bags before I took a nap and took my key off his key chain. He looks down at suitcases beside me. "Monika, really? Baby, you going to do this shit now?" He reaches for me but barely grazes my arm. "This real fucked up! Damn! Why you tripping right now?"

"No, don't touch me. Look, I'm done Gio. Time for you to go. Maybe one of your boys can let you stay with them." That was petty. I didn't have to say that.

Just in case this goes sideways, I make my way into the closet for clothes. He has never been physical, but this situation could make a man flip. I turn to open a drawer for a shirt. At the threshold of the closet door, Gio stares at me in disbelief. Nearing tears, he belligerently says, "You know what, I knew you weren't happy. But I thought we could get pass it. Damn Mon, so you been made up your mind a long time ago! Why the fuck you choose tonight though? You cold as fuck you know that right?" He pauses. His voice grows louder. "I should fuck you. Ain't nobody gonna do to you what I do. You really just gone let this go?"

He holds his dick in his hand. Again, from absolute habit, I peer down to see the partially erect dick in his hand.

"Gio, you are not the only man with good dick. For real, don't drag this out. Can you just get your stuff and go?"

Gio stumbles into the closet. His body trapping me against the built-in shelves. He reeks of alcohol. He lowers his voice a few octaves. "You didn't even get fucked tonight. Let me fuck you one last time and I'll leave."

"That's not a good idea—" Before I could finish my sentence, he leans down and kisses me, pressing his body against mine. I drop the shirt in my hand. "Gio, we shouldn't . . . you should . . ." My body contradicts my words. His hands reach around me unhooking my bra, ripping it off me. He then roughly pulls off my panties. I should say stop, but the words are stuck in my throat. He pulls my arm, leading us from the closet to the bedroom. I trip over shoes to keep up with him. He aggressively bends me over the bed, quickly taking out his dick and entering me from behind. So much for whiskey dick. I wait for him to stroke me. He simply rests his dick deep in my pussy while gripping and smacking my ass. My pussy contracts around him, squeezing him tightly. "Umm!" I moan.

"Knew you wanted this," Gio says.

His hands run from my ass up my back. He then lifts me up by the back of my neck. "Gio!" I gasp. My back now pressed against his chest. He kisses me with hunger, then bends me back over the bed. Still, I wait for him to stroke me. Again, he simply rests his dick deep in my pussy. He releases my hair from the high bun. He wraps my braids around his fist and pulls lightly. Again, my pussy tugging on his dick. Damn, why is the sex so damn good! He pulls my hair harder. "Gio, please," I whimper.

He pulls his dick out. "You being a real bitch, Monika. You on some fuck shit," he says before re-entering. His strokes are hard and slow. "See how easy that was to get you wet. Tell me you don't like this shit."

Gio's strokes pick up speed. My moans grow louder. "Yes, harder!" The sound of skin-to-skin contact is driving me crazy.

He's tapping my ass hard. I grind my ass up against him, seeking another orgasm. Before I could cum, he grunts and releases inside of me.

Yeah, he's mad, mad. I chuckle to myself. He usually allows me to cum first. Guess he owed me that one. He pulls out and staggers into the bathroom. I replay the surreal events from this night in my head. I throw on light clothing and wait by the bedroom door for him to exit the bathroom. "Gio, come on," I call for him.

He finally exits the bathroom. "Baby, you really want to do this? Let me try to make this right," he says unable to mask his feelings due to the alcohol.

I stare into his eyes, "No, let's not do this dance all night. This for real. Just take your things and go, Gio. Please."

After a few silent minutes, he finally gets the point and picks up his bags. I follow him and watch him descend the stairs. He tells his boys it's time to go. Gio grabs his keys and heads toward the door with one last look back at me. The sadness in his eyes aches my heart. He exits the door, closing it quietly behind him. I stare at the door for minutes before the tears begin to flow. The music is making my headache worse. I bang on the remote until it stops. It was a mistake to turn off the music. The silence reminding me of the new normal of not having Gio here.

I take a deep breath and wipe my eyes, contemplating whether I should run after him. But just as I do, a slight smile creeps on my face. I recall the feeling of Justin's mouth on my pussy.

I say to myself, "Don't do it Mona!"

Blindsided

In the walk-in closet, I remove a navy-blue sweater off the hanger and pull it over my head. The snug fit pairs nicely with the light washed jeans and tan boots I'm wearing. I smooth my hands over my beard. I turn to the side to see how my man's is poking. Pleased with my reflection in the full-length mirror, I exit to the bedroom.

My phone vibrates in my hand. It's my childhood friend, Byron, facetiming me. I answer, "Aye, what the fuck am I doing? Man, this is the craziest shit you have ever talked me into B."

Byron and his wife, Dion, somehow convinced me to go on a blind date with one of her line sisters. Dion is beautiful and smart, but is somewhat of a prude in my eyes. Byron begged Dion to set me up with someone. I believe, no, *I know* he's tired of me not being able to hang out with him and Dion without being a third wheel. He probably means well, but I don't understand why they assumed a blind date was the best idea. Granted, I don't always choose the best companion. And yes, maybe I'm attracted to drama, but there's no way this is it.

Byron laughs, "Don, you've done far worse than a blind date. Trust. I know you remember that time in Vegas…"

A scowl quickly covers my face. "Aye, B…. Yo, not tonight, bruh. Don't bring that up."

Byron teases me often about a trip to Las Vegas four years ago. At the time, we were both bachelors and thought a guy's trip would be a good idea. Upon arrival at the hotel, we were already on a level seven. With luggage in tow, we gambled in the casino having one-to-many drinks before we even checked in. Once we made it to the room, we showered to hit the strip and continue our weekend of self-destruction. After leaving the club extremely intoxicated, we walked the strip back to the hotel. Along the way, I saw this good-looking woman sitting by the fountains. Of course, in my inebriated state, any woman was probably my type. Byron kept pulling my arm to keep walking, but I resisted. At some point he gives in, but insisted on laughing hysterically the entire walk back to the hotel. The woman and I went to the room and had sex; I think. I blacked out before we got back to the room. I woke the next morning with a massive hangover to find Bryon wide awake on the other bed staring at me.

"Damn, what the fuck happened last night?" I asked. Byron looked at me with disgust. He opened his mouth to speak, but closed it. What is he not saying? "Yo, what the fuck?"

Byron shook his head. "Dude, you don't remember?"

I stand from the bed in search of water. "Yeah, I remember taking shots, walking back from the club and talking to some girl."

He explodes in laughter. "Bro, you slept with a homeless woman last night!" His laughter could no longer be contained. He was bent over crying and attempting to catch his breath. I wanted to tackle him for making up a fucked up crazy story, but my feet felt like they were weighted by bricks.

"B, stop playing." My whole entire being hoped he was telling some sick joke. The lie rolled so easily from his lips.

"I swear to you. I'll show you. Look!" Byron pulled out his phone and scrolled. He finally stood from the bed and walked over to me. He showed me a zoomed in picture of me and the woman from last night. She was smiling happily. Her hair was a mess and her clothes looked a bit tattered. He then zoomed out and showed her standing by a grocery cart filled with her belongings. The remainder of the weekend was a blur. I couldn't get over that night. I vowed to never visit Las Vegas, ever again.

$$\infty \infty \infty$$

A couple passes me on the sidewalk, showing a little too much PDA in my opinion. I nervously wait outside of the restaurant for the blind date to arrive. Dion mentioned her friend is from Chicago and recently moved to Los Angeles. Besides her name, that's the extent of what I know about her.

A voice from behind rips me from my thoughts. "Dontario?"

Here goes nothing! I turn around to see what unexciting prize I've won tonight. The first thing I notice is bright red lipstick. "Leannah?" I ask.

"Yes! How are you?" Leannah leans in for a brief hug.

Quickly, my eyes scan her from head to toe. I attempt to check her out without it being obvious. She's cute in a black dress with gold stuff on it and gold heels with straps, but not my usual type. I like em' thick, with a fat ass and cute face. In that order. Leannah is petite. She reminds me of a girl I dated in high school. No body at all. This is not starting off well for me. With a lack of enthusiasm, I reply, "I'm good. How about you?"

Leannah smiles. Her white teeth glow brightly against the red lipstick. I mean she does have nice lips. They're not too big, not too small. No lie, I'd kiss them if given the chance.

She says, "I'm okay. It's really nice to meet you, Dontario. I wasn't sure what to expect."

"Me neither. You look nice tonight."

She responds, "Thank you. I like the blue sweater. The color looks good on you."

Of course, the sweater looks good against my butter pecan skin, but to receive the compliment is nice. With that unexpected confidence boost, a sense of calmness covers me. "Thank you. Ready to go in?"

"Please! I'm so hungry."

"Really?" She skinny as hell. I laugh internally and open the restaurant door for Leannah to enter.

"Um yeah, we are having dinner, right?" She giggles. "I looked at the menu last night and I'm excited to try this place."

What type of nerdy shit is that? I nod anyway. "So, you haven't been here before? I thought you chose this place."

"No, this is my first time. I thought you chose it." I shake my head no. The hostess grabs two menus and leads us to our table. We take our seats and order two waters to start.

Leannah asks, "Who do you think chose this place? With it being Japanese, I would say Dion did."

Without looking up from the drink menu, I reply, "Nah, probably Byron. He like this kind of stuff." An awkward silence rest between us. I read over the drink menu for the third time, still unsure of what to order. I need something to liven my spirits. I ask Leannah, "You know what you want to drink?"

Her eye contact is direct, yet she quickly lowers her head to view the menu. Ha! She think she slick. I caught her checking me out.

"Do you want to do sake? Might as well do it right." She turns her menu around and points out the different sake to me. Does she think I'm slow or stupid? Aren't they all the same?

"Sake is cool." I try to hide my annoyance at her bossy nature. She probably doesn't even know how irritating that is. I'd be rude to mention it, especially since I don't plan to see her again. Although, I would definitely smash if she giving it up. With that thought, I'm beginning to appreciate the simplicity of blind dating. No expectations, plus she doesn't have my contact information. It's a win-win situation for me.

The waitress approaches our table finally breaking the silence between Leannah and I. "Hi I'm Amelia. How are you all? Is there anything to get you started tonight?"

Leannah smiles at me. Guess that's my cue. I look to the waitress, "We'll start with the sake."

The waitress asks, "Do you know which one?" My eyes dart from the waitress to Leannah, back to the waitress like a dumbass.

"The Yaegaki Nigori will be fine." Leannah comes through in the clutch. I had no idea what the waitress asked me. It was like she was speaking foreign. The waitress scribbles on her notepad. "Great choice. Is there anything else? Maybe a starter?"

Leannah turns the page in her menu. "An order of the edamame and... the shumai. Dontario, anything you want to try?"

The menu has stared at me these past ten minutes. Japanese is not my first choice of cuisine. You can give me a steakhouse or a burger joint any day though. Leannah looks so comfortable that it makes me uncomfortable. She's probably internally laughing at me for not being cultured. I respond with the only thing I can remember, "Umm, just some steamed dumplings."

"Okay, got it. I'll get this started. If you need anything else, please let me know." She departs the table.

I look across the table at Leannah. She's still looking over the menu. "Thanks for the assist. Yeah, I don't know too much about this kinda stuff. Appreciate you helping me out."

She smiles at me, flashing her bright smile again. "No problem. Dion and I used to eat Japanese all the time in college, so I know enough to get by. You know I would love to visit Japan one day."

"Oh, really?" My conversation is intentionally dry. At this point I would rather her lead the conversation, so I can just eat and chill. But my plan to fuck her tonight must have intercepted my ability to act uninterested. Conquering a woman like Leannah could be a satisfying feat.

"Yes, traveling is fun. It's enlightening. I love going new places." Leannah nods her head and continues scanning over the menu, giving me time to observe her. Her face is cute and her skin complexion is soft brown like a stuffed teddy bear. She has big eyes with long lashes. The twisted hairstyle that looks likes dreadlocs are long and fall down her back. The eyebrow piercing doesn't quite fit, but who am I to say.

I ask, "You just moved here, right?"

"Yes, from Chicago."

The waitress approaches us and places the sake and edamame on the table. "Here you are. The rest of your order will be out soon. Is there anything else I can get for you?"

Leannah swings the twists over her shoulder. "Yes, but we'll wait for the rest of the appetizers."

The waitress exits the table. Leannah bows her head and says a quick prayer. She lifts her head and looks directly at me. She doesn't ask why I'm staring; she just reaches for the little sake cups pouring for us both.

I pick up my glass and hold it up. "To blind dates?"

She grins and lifts her glass, "To blind dates."

After dinner we walked the Third Street Promenade in Santa Monica. Surprisingly, the conversation flowed easily between us over dinner. Probably because we nearly finished the entire bottle of sake.

We laughed and talked about some of everything from travel, to work, to life goals. Leannah became more interesting throughout dinner. I'd prefer to have her in my bed for a night cap, but I don't think she's the type to give it up tonight based on the conversation. Yeah, we flirted a little over dinner. She fed me sushi, complimented my looks. Not to mention, I caught her staring at my mouth a couple of times. Even after all of that, women will hit you with the 'this was fun' line at the end of the night. So, I'm not getting my hopes up.

I ask, "So, where did you park?"

Leannah stops and looks at me with her head tilted. "Getting rid of me already? Wow. Thought the night was young."

My mouth falls open in shock, "I mean it's still young. Tell me. What would you like to do, Leannah?"

"I don't know if you'd be up for it." Leannah teases.

"What? You wanna fuck?" I blurt out unashamed. That may have been too forward, but who cares. Her head falls back in deep laughter, causing me to smile harder than I'd like. "Why is that so funny?"

Leannah laughs so hard she needs to catch her breath. "It's funny because I didn't expect you to say that."

"For a sec, I thought you were offended."

"Why would I be? Unless… you would just fuck anything. Now, then I would feel some type of way."

"Hmph!" It's a good thing she don't know about Vegas. Leannah's starting to grow on me. We turn around and begin walking back towards the restaurant.

She stops walking and looks up at me. The apprehensive lines in her forehead concern me. "I've been wanting to go the dispensary since I've moved here, but didn't want to go alone. You know Dion is not going near anywhere or anyone that sells drugs."

I chuckle at her fact about Dion. "Yeah, she a little uptight."

"You down or what?" She playfully leans into my arm.

This could be my *in* to go back to her place. I contemplate my original plan of going home to play NBA 2K. But why would I pass up new pussy? Guess I just answered my own question. This chick has thrown me for a loop all night with her unpredictability.

"I'm wit it. There's actually one on Lincoln not too far from here."

Leannah dances a quick shimmy in her heels. Okay, she does have nice legs! Now if only she had some ass.

Leannah swipes a card to open the parking garage gate to her condo building in Marina Del Ray. She sticks her arms out of the window and points to the visitor parking. After I follow her through the gate, I park and meet her near the elevators. We make our way upstairs to her condo. She definitely making real money. The condo is fucking nice! Marble floors, ocean views, and a big ass kitchen. I'm stunned walking through the massive space. It's a mansion compared to my studio apartment in Chinatown.

"Still unpacking?" Moving boxes are scattered throughout the living area and hallway. I walk over to the ocean facing windows. The Pacific Ocean is dark and hidden under the moon. The views during the day are probably insane.

"Yeah. Sorry for the mess. I've been so busy with work." Leannah retreats to the other side of the condo.

I yell to her from the living room. "Your place is nice."

Leannah returns to the open living space. "Thank you. Do you think you can roll up for me? I'm not that good at it."

I tease her, "You want to smoke and don't know how to roll. Priorities Leannah…"

"It's sad, right? Hey, do you want something to drink?" She's in the kitchen before I respond.

"Yeah, just some water." Leannah pours two glasses of water and stands at the other end of the table. She studies my movements breaking down the package she bought.

"How about I put on some music." She exits down the hallway again. Within a few minutes, soft music seeps through the surround speakers. I finish rolling up the joint and clean up the residue. She still hasn't returned to the dining room. I pat my pockets and look around for a lighter. I settle on next option by going to her gas stove and to light it. I take a long hit and wander down the hallway with a trail of smoke behind me. As I approach her bedroom, I stop at the door opening. "Damn!"

Leannah lies across the bed in black lingerie with her twists now pulled back into a ponytail. The view is enticing, and I'm not talking about the ocean. Leannah smiles, "Took you long enough."

"You put me to work, and left." Gradually, I step further into the bedroom. Leannah scoots to the far side of the bed and waves me over. That damn good girl façade is fading away bit by bit. Why she trying to make me like her? The game plan is to fuck, leave, and hope I never hear from her again. Right? I try to remind myself why I'm here.

I sit down on the bed, lie back against the pillows with my shoes hanging over the side of the bed. I take another hit and pass it to her. She inspects it and takes a hit, coughing a little as the smoke hits her lungs. Now, I know she on one, because my handiwork is A-1. "Did you really just inspect my work? You can't be asking for my assistance and then hate on it," I say teasingly.

Leannah playfully shoves me back, then climbing on top to straddle me. "I'm not hating. I'm admiring." She bats her lashes and smirks.

I gently massage her thighs to feel her out. In response, she smiles and takes another hit of the joint. I watch her inhale and exhale. She turns the joint around and brings the fire end up to her mouth.

I blurt out, "Aye, what you..." She leans forward and blows a shotgun to my face. I suck in the stream of smoke until my lungs are full. I hold it for a few seconds before releasing. I cough and my dick hardens instantly. It didn't take long for Leannah to notice, because she leans over to nightstand and dabs out the joint.

My hand grips her chin to guide her mouth to mine. We share an unhurried kiss. Our tongues dance to a slow sweet song. Every touch is slow and melodic. Maybe I'm just high, but everything we're doing has purpose. From the way she rolls her hips against me to the way she sucks my tongue. I palm her small ass, damn near lifting her to ceiling. I roll over and lay her down on her back. She helps me remove my sweater and undershirt. I kick off my boots, immediately returning my mouth to hers. My hands explore her body. Her skin is smooth and soft to the touch. I can't help but to taste the places my hands have explored. My tongue leaves a trail of wet kisses to her neck, her collarbone, her shoulder.

Leannah massages my ears while I explore her body. I didn't even know my ears were an erogenous zone. Whatever she's doing has the blood pumping straight to my dick. I stand briefly to remove a condom from my pocket and step out of my jeans before climbing back on top of her. I dry hump her, grinding my full length against her causing her to moan. I reach my hands into her panties to find her wet and ready. She lifts her hips assisting me to remove her panties.

With one hand I remove my briefs and put on protection. I guide my dick into her wetness. Her pussy cozy ass fuck! I'm talking pillows by the fireplace. The weed has me moving slow as hell. I couldn't rush even if I wanted to. I slow grind the shit out of her warm pussy. It must've been good to her too because she starts rolling her hips against me. I bite my bottom lip and stick my thumb in her mouth. Her pussy walls grip me tight. Oh, she like this shit! After a few more pumps, I pull out and roll her over on her stomach. I snap off her bra and watch her throw it to the floor.

She toots her lil ass up for me to enter. We're at it again. I slowly ride her ass. Swear, I can't remember the last time I've rolled my hips this much. I might need to fuck high more often.

Leannah moans, "Umm! It feels so good!"

I grip her waist and grind harder. She's right, this shit feels so good. I could do this all night. You know that feeling when you jacking off and you don't want it to end. Yeah, that way.

"Yeah! I flip her on her side and slow stroke her pussy. I lick my thumb and press it against her asshole. She moans and grinds her hips against me. My thumb breaks the entrance. I push it in as far as it will go. She hooks her arm underneath her thigh and pulls her knee to her chest. She licks her hand and begins to rub her clit. I grip her ass like a bowling ball. I watch my dick enter in, then out of her again, and again, and again. I watch her play with herself.

She says, "Yes, Dontario! I want you to cum in my mouth!"

Damn, what she just say! I try counting down. Fifty, forty-nine, forty-eight, forty-seven...

All I can think about is cumming in her mouth. I flip her back over onto her stomach and ride her slow again to prolong my erection. Just as I get comfortable, she closes her thighs together. Now, why the fuck she do that? My dick slides in and out her tight wet fold.

Sunsets, soccer, sandals... I try to think about anything else other than coming. That's until she begins rolling her hips in a circle. "Fuck!"

I try to steady my strokes, but it's not working. My concentration is on trying to keep a rhythm, but I can't. She's taken control and I don't know how to get that shit back.

I tap her shoulder, "Come here." I pull out and force her to turn over. I continue stroking my dick with my hand, while Leannah hurries onto her knees in front of me. She places her tongue on the head of my dick waiting expectantly for my seed. My body tingles all over. I feel like I'm about to nut, but the release doesn't come instantly like usual. It slowly courses through my body. It tingles from my feet up to my chest. An explosion of cum shoots from my dick causing me to damn near miss my target.

"Aaahh FUCK!" A loud grunt escapes me. I fill her open mouth with my unborn children. She swallows and takes my dick into her mouth, milking me whatever's left. Exhausted, I collapse on the bed with my right hand holding my heart.

I think aloud, "What the fuck was that?"

My heart beats wildly in my chest as I attempt to catch my breath. That was the best feeling I've had in my entire fucking life. I felt that orgasm in my soul. I'm astounded, whatever that means. That shit sounds right though. I don't want this moment to end. Shit, I like it here.

Leannah asks, "What was what?"

There's no way I can tell her I'm about to fuck up her life. I can't tell her that every time I fuck, I'll be a damn addict chasing that high again. Or that I underestimated her, or that I was blindsided by a fucking blind date.

Instead, I roll on my side and pull her body into mine. She spoons her little bit of ass snug against me. I whisper in her ear with a devious grin on my face. "Nothing."

Fate of Love

The restaurant is busy, filled with late-night patrons. The hostess shows them to their table for four. The dining area is bursting with chattering voices and the clinking of silverware against plates. Quinton and Jayce greet their friends, Chivon and Danny, as they approach the table. Quinton pulls the chair from the table for Jayce to sit.

Quinton takes his seat. He asks Danny, "What's good my man? How y'all been?"

"We've been good. Thanks for inviting us out to celebrate."

Chivon chimes in, "Yes, we needed a night out from the kids. It's nice to get dressed up for a change. How's it going for you all? Happy Anniversary to you by the way!"

"Thank you so much. I must say, things are well." Jayce flashes Quinton a bright smile. Quinton responds by lovingly squeezing Jayce's thigh under the table.

This day marks Quinton and Jayce's third wedding anniversary. April 9th will forever be a day they cherish. It's the day when the fate of two separate lives forever changed.

Jayce eyes her husband, witnessing his immeasurable beauty.

"What?" Quinton notices his wife watching him closely.

"Nothing! You're just so damn fine tonight. Can't help but stare."

Quinton smiles. If not for the dark tone of his skin, you could see the redness flush his face. "The way you look in that dress. It reminds me of that dress you wore when we first met." He stares off in a wondering gaze and bites his bottom lip recalling the tight white dress she wore that night.

"You remembered what I was wearing?"

"Could never forget. I wanted you the minute I first laid on eyes on you."

Jayce rolls her eyes. "That is so cliché. For me… it wasn't clear until the second date." Quinton shows Jayce a mimicking scowl. "I'm kidding. I remember that day like it just happened."

They all share a light-hearted laugh. Chivon asks, "How did y'all meet anyway? I know it was at the bar, but I've never heard the details."

Quinton and Jayce lock eyes and smile. Jayce responds first, "Well I remember the night going something like this . . ."

Jayce

My phone vibrates against the bathroom counter. I look down at the display to see Lydia, my best friend, is calling. "Damn, what she want now. I just spoke to her five minutes ago."

I put the phone on speaker. "Hey girl, what's up?"

"Jay, why that red top I wanted to wear got a stain on it? I'm so pissed. Now I gotta figure out a whole new outfit. This night is on my nerves already."

"Oh damn, sorry girl. As much as you shop, you gots to have something in that big ass closet. Didn't you tell me you were picking me up at 8 o'clock? Lyd it's 6:30 already. You better figure it out!"

"I know, I'm about to get in the shower now. Let me ravage through this damn closet." She sighs. "I'll call you when I pull up."

"Okay. See you in a bit."

I start the shower to warm the water before stepping in. A Friday night out is much needed for us both. She's a cosmetologist and make-up artist. I'm a marketing strategist for a new online-based company. Work has been hectic, and we haven't seen each other in nearly two weeks. That's a long time for friends of over ten years. We met in our senior year of high school. We attended two separate schools but shared some of the same friends. I was with my then-boyfriend at a house party hosted by one of his friends. My boyfriend started an argument that night. He became angry with me for wearing a pair of short shorts—definitely some high school drama. I was so pissed I didn't talk to his ass for the rest of the night. I ended up laughing and chatting with Lydia for like an hour. It turned out Lydia lived two blocks over from my family's home. Since that night, we've grown to become close friends.

After a relaxing shower, I pull my freshly washed, natural hair back into a low bun. I tame my edges and grab a scarf to tie my hair down while I finish getting dressed. For me, this is a 'natural make-up' kind of night. Starting by applying a little under-eye concealer, taming my eyebrows, and applying heavy mascara. Finishing the look with a natural pink lip gloss. Pleased with my work, I head to the closet to find something to wear. Because I'm not in the mood for a bunch of hungry, prying eyes, I settle on a sexy, relaxed look with a white racerback knee-length dress and a pair of tan peep-toe heels, accessorizing with bohemian ear-rings and bangles. I look at my phone and have about 15 minutes to spare-or so I thought. A new text message pops up.

Lydia: I'm outside. Hurry ur ass up
Me: otw down

I ride the elevator down from the 5th floor. Exiting the lobby door, I spot Lydia's white SUV in a designated visitor parking spot.

She rolls down the window and yells, "Come on girl, so we can find decent parking!" She's so extra, and I love her for it.

"Damn, you see me. I'm right here," I laugh. I enter the car on the passenger side and lean over to hug Lydia. She's driving off before I even buckle my seatbelt.

"You looking good girl. See I knew you would pull something together. Loving this long hair on you too! You making me feel underdressed though." She is looking way sexier than I in a strapless red mini dress and 6-inch black stilettos. "We still going to Q-Bar, right?"

"Yes girl! You know they have the best drinks. Plus, that's where all the men who work downtown go after work on Fri-days. And you know I need to get some." She looks over at me with a 'you know I ain't lying' look.

We find an unmetered parking spot near the bar entrance. After exiting the car, a younger guy stops us before we can get inside. "Y'all looking good. What's yo name?" he asks Lydia. He appears way too young to be at any bar. His extremely tight pants sag around his butt and he sports a shadowed mustache. Lydia smiles at him and tells him she's too old for him.

We make our way inside. The first time we visited Q-Bar, we got so drunk we had to rideshare back to my place to crash. Hopefully, this time is different because I have shit to do tomorrow.

The DJ is playing a smooth neo-soul mix. It's somewhat crowded with mostly men in dress shirts and business suits. Ten to fifteen people occupy the dance floor. The dim lighting, exposed bricks, and black painted walls are masculine yet cozy. "I really like this place. The vibe is always so chill here," Lydia says as we survey for a table.

"Over there," I point. "Looks like a table is open by the dance floor." I lead us past the bar top tables towards the smaller two top tables. As we take our seats, I ask, "Did you see that guy at the bar with the green shirt?" I look over to find him looking our way.

Lydia turns over her shoulder to take a peek, "Ooh girl, he fine! The dude next to him fine too." She scoots her chair in. "Told you they be up in here."

"What you drinking tonight? I'm not getting super drunk like we did last time. Took me all weekend to recover from that night." A few drinks and some dancing are about all I can handle tonight. This week has been longer than an old lady's titties.

A young waiter approaches our table to take our orders. Lydia states, "We'll start with two green tea shots, please." I look at her with wide eyes. She looks back at me with raised eyebrows.

"What? It would have taken you all day to figure out what you wanted." I shake my head at her remark, partly because it's true. We share an extended laugh.

I look over towards Green Shirt Guy again, "Girl, if this man keeps looking over here—"

"You gone do what! Let that man look. He wants you and ain't said two words to you. You better handle it too with your conservative ass! I don't know why you be turning them fine ass men down all the time. Jay, you been single too long." I roll my eyes her way, knowing she's right.

A few moments later, the waiter returns with our shots. "What we drinking to Lyd?" She shrugs her shoulders, "How about we cheer to the weekend!" We clink our glasses together and drink the sweet smooth liquid in a single swallow. Lydia excitedly claps and lifts her fists in the air.

"So, what's the deal with you and Andre?" I ask Lydia. She mentioned they haven't spoken in the past week. I assume it had something to do with his club promoting job, but she never said. They've been dating for the past five months after meeting at a nightclub.

Lydia shrugs her shoulders. "Girl, I don't even want to talk about him. He acting so damn shady. Feel like I'm wasting my time with him. You know how it is when the newness fade."

I nod. "Yes, those first few months be fun as hell. Well don't waste your time. That's no good for anybody."

The waiter approaches our table with another round of shots. Lydia asks, "What's this? We didn't order these…"

"The gentleman at the bar sent these to you." The waiter looks over his shoulder. "Would you like for me to take them back?"

"Hell naw, we'll take 'em," Lyd says with no shame. She moves the other shot glasses out of the way before raising her glass to the Green Shirt Guy. With a slight smile, I do the same.

"Could you bring us two waters, please?" I ask the waiter. I observe the room, taking in the atmosphere. A few people are dancing, some are chatting, and others are surveying the room as well.

Lydia starts to dance in her seat.

"Jay, I'm so glad we got out tonight. I had four different clients today. Seems like I've been around the whole damn city. My last make-up appointment was at four for this girl going to some charity event. Girl, I need this night."

"That's def a busy day. We gone make sure you have a fun night then."

She raises her hand to high five me. "Yesss! Come on let's go dance!" Hell, why not. We grab our purses and head over to the small crowded dance floor. Lauryn Hill's 'Everything is Everything' is playing. We're both dancing to the music enjoying the buzz from the alcohol. I close my eyes and settle into my own groove.

A few moments later, a hand touches my arm. Quickly, I open my eyes, expecting to see Lyd. To my surprise, it's Green Shirt Guy. I look at him intensely, finally getting to see him up close. He has dark almond-shaped eyes, sexy full lips, and a defined jawline. His skin is the color of chocolate syrup. Damn, am I staring? I should probably say something.

He leans in and whispers in my ear, "Mind if join you?" With reservation, I nod my head. His eyes penetrate my soul while he reaches for my hand. He presses his hard body against mine. He is so fine! My heart races and there is an anxiousness being this close to him. He moves in a sensual side to side sway. Finally, he asks, "What's your name, beautiful?"

I clear my throat, "It's Jayce and yours?"

"Jayce," he repeats my name in a deep sexy tone. "My name is Quinton. You enjoying yourself tonight?" His hand landing on the small of my back.

"Yes, it's good so far. I was having a nice little moment before you interrupted me though," I say with a smirk on my face.

He holds me tighter. "Oh really, I apologize. Let me make it up to you. Buy you another drink?"

"You're not trying to get me drunk, are you?"

"Of course not. Just trying to say I'm sorry."

"Fine. But only one more." Quinton takes my hand and leads me through the crowd. I tap Lydia on the shoulder and point to the bar to let her know where to find me.

We approach the bar, and the bartender hurries over. "Another for me and a green tea shot for the lady," Quinton says.

"Thank you for the drinks earlier. That was nice of you."

He leans in, "No problem. I had to find a reason to talk to you tonight. I noticed you before you walked in the door."

Okay, he's really trying to get in my pants. "Really? Sounds like I'm your prey tonight."

He laughs, "No not like that. I happened to be watching the door and saw you and your girl standing outside. Was hoping you were actually coming inside."

"And if I wouldn't have come in, you would have done what?"

"I don't know. I don't have to worry about that now," he says as he stares into my eyes.

I look away to hide my blushing. He's way too damn sexy. Good looks and good conversation. I tell myself to be careful with this one.

The bartender delivers our drinks. Quinton's drink is a clear liquid with a lime garnish. He hands me the shot, "Cheers?"

"What are we drinking to Quinton?"

He bites his bottom lip, "Cheers to a good night."

We clink our glasses. He sips while I shoot my green tea shot.

"Come on Jayce. Dance with me." He ushers me back toward the dance floor.

Lydia is still on the floor grooving with some good-looking white dude that's well into his fifties. "Okay girl!" I say in passing.

Quinton spins me into his arms. His hard chest presses against my back and his warm breath against my neck. We slow dance to an unfamiliar song. He deliberately runs his hands from the dip of my waist, over my hips, down to my thighs. His unexpected touch freezes me instantly. I turn to face him, informing him I need to use the restroom.

He slow nods. "Okay, I'll be here."

I walk down a long hallway past the men's restroom, turning right, around a corner to the women's restroom. Upon entering the restroom, I take my time. I contemplate how to handle this man. He's intoxicating, or maybe it's those shots. No, it can't just be the alcohol as I remember he had my attention when we first entered the bar. I wash my hands and reapply my lip gloss in the mirror. "Okay girl, you got this," I say to myself.

I exit the restroom and see him standing there. "What are you doing?"

"I don't know to be honest. I'm just drawn to you. I wasn't too forward earlier, was I?"

If I wasn't so interested, this would've been creepy. He doesn't seem like the type to sweat any woman. His looks and demeanor alone could get any woman's attention. I want him and I know it. I give in by leaning in to kiss him. That may have been all the invitation he needed. He leans in closer, kissing me with hunger. Quinton looks down the hallway to see if the coast is clear. He gently turns me around and presses me against the wall. His right hand rubs my shoulder and he whispers in my ear, "I've been wanting to touch you all night. Your nipples spoke to me before you did." His hands slide over my shoulder underneath the fabric of my dress. He palms my C-cup and places my nipple between his fingers, eagerly applying light pressure.

"Ahh," a loud moan escapes my lips, grateful the pounding music drowns my indiscretions. The butterflies in my pussy are fluttering uncontrollably. He places his left hand around my neck and tilts my head back. His growing erection against my ass gives me chills. And he has a big dick! Who is this man? This night cannot be real!

He must have noticed my thoughts wandering. He snaps me back in the moment by teasing me with light kisses on my neck and squeezing my nipple again. I should stop this before I lose control. On cue, he removes his hand from my dress as a patron exits the restroom. Quickly, I turn around to say, "I should go check on my girl."

"Like that?" The lines in his forehead are present. "Okay. Don't leave though, Jayce. I need a couple of minutes." He looks down at his crotch. My eyes follow his to see he's covering his hard-on. A huge smile covers my face.

I shake off my naughty thoughts and exit down the long hallway. I spot Lydia at our table. She's with the cute guy who sat next to Quinton earlier at the bar. "Oh, hey girl, where you been?" she asks.

"Hey, you good?" I ask.

The cute guy stands to offer me his seat. I thank him and take it.

"Jay, this is Kellen. Kellen, this is my girl Jayce." We offer a polite smile to one another.

"Nice to meet you."

Lydia says, "Jay, the guy you were dancing with earlier is the owner of the bar."

"Really? Hmph. He didn't mention that." Guess he was too busy feeling me up.

Kellen says, "Well, I hope y'all are having a good time. Glad y'all came out." His southern charm on full display. The eye contact between him and Lydia is strong. I feel as if I interrupted something.

"Would y'all like something from the bar?" he asks.

"Thanks, a water for me."

"I'll have another green tea shot and a water. Thank you, Kellen," Lydia says. He turns leaving us at the table alone. A few minutes pass before Lydia or I speak.

"Damn, how many shots have you had? There's like four more shot glasses on the table?" I ask Lydia.

"Hold up, know you not talking. I seen you with the owner taking shots earlier. Where you been anyway? Y'all snuck off somewhere."

We both laugh. My thoughts flash back to his dick pressed against my ass. "I just went to the restroom. His name is Quinton by the way and I can't believe he's the owner. The name Q-Bar makes sense now."

In my line of sight, Quinton exits the wall separating the bar and the restroom. He comes straight towards our table.

"How you doing?" he says to Lydia.

Kellen is also heading back our way with drinks. "I'm good Mr. Quinton. I'm Lydia. How are you?" she says before I could introduce them.

Quinton looks directly at me. "I'm good. Thank y'all for coming out. Has my boy been taking care of you?"

Lydia blurts, "Yeess! Your boy trying to get it! Aye!" She sticks out her tongue like a panting dog.

"Jayce, can I talk to you for a minute?" he says, blatantly ignoring Lydia's outburst.

I look at Quinton quizzingly before grabbing my purse. "Lydia, I'll be right back." I follow him to the other side of the bar. He stops at a door near the rear of the bar and removes keys from his pocket. He opens the door, steps aside and motions for me to enter. Halfheartedly, I step inside and watch him close the door. The space appears to be his office. It's actually nicer than I would have expected. I assumed bar offices looked like a janitor closet with file cabinets. It's organized and clean. To my surprise, there are actual artworks and plaques on the wall.

He takes a seat behind the desk. "Have a seat," he points to the chair opposite of his desk. Dismissive of his suggestion, I continue standing by the door, annoyed with how much I want him. With pursed lips I say, "So, what did you need to talk about Quinton?"

"To be honest, I wanted to hear what more your body has to say. You keep running from me. No matter what comes out of your sexy little mouth. Your body says you want me."

"Is that so? You brought me all the way to your office to tell me that?"

He shakes his head. "Am I lying? You a handful, you know that. So, you not the least bit curious about what could be? If this could be something more than just physical attraction? I know I want you. Tell me what you want Jayce."

Feeling uncomfortable, I look down at my feet. "How am I supposed to trust what might be temporary lustful feelings? Plus, I've had a few too many shots to be sure of anything right now. It's crazy that you seem so sure of whatever this is! Am I attracted and physically turned on by you? Yes! That's not enough for me though." I pause. "Look, I just met you so I'm not expecting anything beyond that."

He responds with conviction, "I know. I understand, but

please don't just dismiss me. There's something about you. I don't want to spend the rest of my life thinking about Jayce, this woman I met at the bar once. What I do know, is this feeling I feel don't come around too often."

I stare into his eyes. Hoping to pick up on any bullshit he's spitting. This man is laying it all out there, and I'm not sure I know how to handle his honesty. Shit, what happened to a low-key fun night out with my girl!

"For real, what do you want Quinton? I really should get back out there to my girl."

"Your girl will be fine. I asked Kellen to look after her. What I want is for you to come over here." His hand taps his lap, motioning where he'd like for me to be. We have an extended stare down. His confidence makes me uncomfortable, but at the same time I want to fuck him. What is happening?

My body chooses the next course of action for me. I take the initiative by walking over to him, placing my purse on his desk. I look down at him and slowly pull my dress up. Quinton, still seated, scoots the chair back against the wall while keeping his eyes locked on mine. His breathing grows irregular as I put my black lace thong on full display. He watches me remove my thong. I say, "You didn't prepare my seat?"

He rushes to stand and pulls me to him, kissing me eagerly. His hands are all over my ass, grabbing and massaging. But then, he abruptly pulls away. "Bend over. Put your hands on the chair Jayce."

Hesitantly, I place my palms flat on the chair as instructed. He pulls a condom from a drawer and places it on the desk. He unbuttons his jeans. To my surprise, he kneels behind me and begins sucking on my pussy. "Quinton," I whisper, "Did you lock the door?"

He darts his tongue in and out of my pussy. His actions are so unexpected that I can no longer control my pussy. It's contracting uncontrollably. Turned on would be an understatement. For the first time ever, I'm about to cum quick as hell. He kisses my ass cheeks before placing his warm tongue flat against my asshole. He applies pressure in a steady beat. Oh my! I'm about to fucking cum. I whimper again, "Quinton, I'm about to cum."

My core tightens. My pussy throbs. The release is hard and euphoric. My legs are weak, and my heart is pounding. I look at him over my shoulder, watching him unzip and lower his pants. My god, it's one of the most gorgeous dicks I've seen. It's hard dark chocolate with beautiful, strong veins. The head is fucking delectable. I need to know how it tastes.

Before he could grab the condom, I turn around and take a seat in the chair, tugging his shirt towards me. I lick the head like it's melting ice cream. He whimpers my name. "Jayce!" I suck him into my mouth. I only get in a few reps before he stops me. "You trying to make me cum? Nah, I need to feel you baby."

He rips open the condom to sheath himself. "You didn't follow my instructions Jayce. What did I tell you to do?" Quinton says in a deep tone. I try my best to think back. My eyes wander back and forth around the room. What did he tell me to do? Quinton shakes his head out of frustration. "See you don't follow directions well. Stand up and bend over. Hands on the chair." As demanded, I stand and bend over. He removes his shirt and puts on the condom. Next, he slowly enters me. He feels so good that my eyes roll back into my head. Quinton exhales a long breath. He takes his time stroking me, slowly removing his dick and re-entering me. Again, he releases a long breath of air.

What is his trying to do to me? I back my ass on to him, looking back to see his reaction. He bites his bottom lip. "Jayce," he says as his pumps pick up speed, "Give me your fucking number. I'm not stopping until you give me your number."

It feels so good that I contemplate saying no. "Jayce, damn baby. Tell me you want me."

"Quinton, please." Pleading, but not really wanting this to be over. I know he wants to cum. "I'll give you my number. I promise."

He grunts loudly and quickly pulls out as he orgasms.

A silent moment passes. We attempt to comprehend what we just did. Funny enough, I think we both knew   we just experienced a forever moment. A moment in time that will never be forgotten or re-created.

I stand to pull down my dress and extend my arm, motioning for him to sit. He stumbles down onto the chair. I gather my panties from the floor and slip them on. Sedated, he watches my every move.

I pick up a pen from the pencil holder and write my number on one of the blank business checks on his desk. I pick up my purse. "Here's my number."

"Good girl," he says.

I walk towards the door. "I'm going to check on my girl now. Thank you for a great night, Quinton."

Present Day . . .

Quinton observes the faces of Chivon and Danny after Jayce explains how they met. They seem stunned at all the details shared from her perspective. Chivon shifts in her seat, "Well damn! That's some story."

Danny grabs Chivon's hand and gives it a light squeeze. The details from Jayce's storytelling possibly changed the tone of the celebratory dinner. The air is sensual and free-flowing.

"Whew. My man!" Danny gives Q a fist pound. "Is that how you remember it?" he asks.

Quinton shrugs. "Something like that." His eyes dart to Jayce. "Baby, I never knew you were nervous that night. You didn't show it."

"Of course, I was nervous. You were fine as hell in that green shirt."

Quinton throws his head back in laughter. "Now, how I remember that day is a little different."

Jayce curiously tilts her head, "Really? Tell us, baby. I'm curious to hear this!"

Quinton

The gym is usually less crowded on Fridays. It's my favorite day to workout. I take a quick break after finishing a final rep on the ropes. I wrap up my two-hour workout by running a few miles on the treadmill. Work and the gym have filled my schedule lately. No lie, it has been a slow month for my personal life. Maybe I should say sexually. The gym has been my girlfriend lately, and she's been getting that work. It's been nearly a year since I opened a bar downtown. I named it Q-Bar after my friends started calling my place 'Q's Bar' after one of my epic house parties years ago. It's a casual hip-hop lounge for happy hour or a night out. We serve drinks and light appetizers, though most people come to drink and dance. The journey has been challenging but definitely worth it. Looking back, I'm not sure how I managed to work as a mortgage broker for all those years.

I wipe down the treadmill and pack up my bag before leaving the gym. Before heading home, I decide to pick up lunch at Rosa's Café. It was one of my go-to spots during the workweek as mortgage broker. Now I only have the chance to visit after leaving the gym when time permits. I head inside and greet Gracie, the owner. "Hi Gracie, how you doing today?"

"Hi Quinton, I'm doing. You want the usual turkey on rye?"

I nod. "Yes, please." She then shouts the order to the kitchen staff.

"How's it going with you? We don't get to see you as often anymore."

I smile, "The bar is going well. We're finally getting a steady flow of business. How's everything been here?"

She fondles with the napkin dispenser. "We've been steady here too. You still single? I could hook you up with my niece, Mariana. She's really pretty."

I chuckle at her brashness. She does this nearly every time I visit. "Thank you, Mrs. Gracie. I appreciate the offer. Work is keeping me busy right now."

"Yeah, yeah. You are way too handsome to be alone Quinton. Next time you come in here I will call her and make you set up a date. Or you'll have to take me out. One or the other," she laughs.

"Okay, next time if I'm not dating, I may take you up on the offer. How's that?" I say, hoping that will get her off my back.

"Deal!" she says excitedly bouncing her shoulders. "Here's you order. It's on the house today." Grace tilts her head. "It's good seeing you, Quinton. Until next time?"

I place a twenty-dollar bill in the tip jar. "Thank you so much. Until next time Gracie. Enjoy the rest of your day."

It's nearing five in the evening by the time I enter my front door. The bar opens at 4:30 PM on weeknights, 2 PM on Saturday, and it's closed on Sunday. My part-time bar manager, Kellen, opens the bar, while I arrive later to close-up at 2 AM. This works better for his schedule since he has children to tuck in. The thought of kids makes me wonder why I waited so long. Does everything change when you hit your thirties? You want to enjoy stable adulthood while still young, yet feel old enough that you should have a wife and kids. Shit's crazy!

I open the door and drop my keys on the counter. After grabbing a water from the fridge and taking a seat on the couch, I turn on the sports channel while I enjoy my sandwich.

The thought of a woman fills my thoughts. I should probably call Natalie to see if she wants to come by the bar tonight. I haven't talked to her in a minute. Nah, she probably got back with her baby daddy. She would have hit me up for some dick by now. Maybe Big Booty Tonya. She's cool, but talking to her is boring as fuck. The conversation is such a struggle it starts to turn me off almost immediately.

It's obvious jerking off this morning wasn't enough for me. Naw, not today. I need to line something up. I finish my sandwich and throw the remnants in the trash. I cross the living area into the bedroom. I remove my clothes and start the shower.

After showering and applying lotion, I settle on wearing a long sleeve green shirt and dark jeans. I spray on cologne and grab a pair of casual boots to finish the look. Lastly, I check myself out in the mirror before heading out the door.

The bar is only a few miles away from my condo. For safety, I drive to the bar. It's usually after 3 AM when I leave, plus I have to drop off the deposits depending on how well we do that night. I park in the reserved spot at the rear exit. I walk through the small kitchen and head directly to my office.

Kellen is staring at the computer screen. "What's up Kellen? How's it looking tonight?"

"What's good Q? It's starting to pick up now. You know how Fridays be. They start to crowd in around seven or so."

"Yeah, think the new DJ is helping with the pick-up too. Thanks for the suggestion, man. That first guy I hired was trash." I jingle the keys in my pocket. "I'm about head up front to see what it's looking like. Lock up when you're done."

"Alright man. Let me plug in these numbers and I'll be out there in little bit."

Taking the few steps from the office to the bar area, I observe the small crowd. The men in business suits are expressively talking with their hands. The music is still low enough to have conversation without yelling over it. Next, I make my way behind the bar to greet the bartenders. "Did you all get the shipment of the glassware today?"

"Yes sir. We're all stocked up. It was tragic last weekend when we ran short on glasses. It got super busy and we didn't expect it," says Joni, the college-aged bartender.

"Good, glad you all are taken care of. Let me know if you need anything else tonight. Don't forget we'll need to take inventory tomorrow before open." I prepare my usual drink of sparkling water with a fresh lime wedge.

I walk over to the other side of the bar and take a seat near the far end, closest to the kitchen. It's the best view to see the entire bar from the door to the dancefloor.

Kellen appears from the restricted area and takes a seat next to me. He asks, "Yo, did you ever hear back from the new wine vendor? They haven't followed up since we sent the estimates Wednesday."

"No, not yet. I'll check back tomorrow or Monday to see if they're ready to draw up a contract. We should be able to get the terms we asked for since we have the sales to back it up." The door opens with a couple of businessmen entering the bar. I freeze, "Who is that?" A thick, brown-skinned woman stands outside the bar. I say a silent prayer in hopes she's coming inside. I elbow Kellen and nod towards the door. He follows my eyes and turns towards the door.

We watch as she and a light-skinned woman open the door and enter the bar. She's wearing a tight white dress with her hair pulled back. Those curves look dangerous. Damn! Curves is not wearing a bra either. Her nipples are on full display. She's too damn sexy to be out of the house looking like that. Especially with my hormones on ten today.

Kellen turns to me, "Okay my boy, haven't seen you act like this in a while. Calm down dog."

"Yeah, shorty in the white dress definitely got my attention." I watch her and the light-skinned woman in the red dress find a table near the dancefloor. They take their seats and Curves is right in my line of view. I watch her look my way.

She definitely noticed me. I lean back on the stool. "Kel, I gotta figure out a way to talk to her tonight. Ain't trying to be 'that dude', ya know. She fine as hell."

Kellen laughs and shakes his head, "Uh oh, she got you trippin, Q. Just send her a drink or something!"

"I mean that could work." Kellen's right. I'll wait until they order and send another round on the house.

Kellen taps my arm, "Aye, I'm going to check on the door."

I nod to him and turn my attention back to Curves. They finally order drinks. I stop Brian, their waiter, as he makes his rounds checking on his other tables. "What did the lady in the white dress order?"

He replies, "Sir, they ordered green tea shots." The staff are too formal for my liking. No matter how many times, being called 'sir' took some getting used to.

"Brian, when you're done making your rounds. Please send another round to their table. On me."

"Sure thing," he responds. I thank him and let him get back to his job.

I'm not sure what it is about this woman. I haven't worked this hard for a woman's attention in a long while. Women usually throw themselves at me, that's until lately. Or maybe I've been giving off the wrong vibes. I'll wait for her to accept the drinks before I make my next move.

I observe the room again, trying to revert my attention elsewhere. The businessmen are getting loose and making their way to the dancefloor. The DJ is playing upbeat neo-soul. Similar to my house parties, the vibe is chill and relaxing. Later tonight the younger people will crowd in for drinks before club-hopping into the early morning. Around eleven, the DJ will play hip-hop to liven the bar.

Brian approaches Curves' table with the shots I ordered. Brian, Curves, and the red dress woman all look my way. I grow slightly nervous, wondering if she'll accept. I fidget, spinning the glass in my hand. The woman in the red dress looks in my direction, raising her glass. Curves smiles and raises her glass, so I raise my glass and smile back, "Yea, I got you."

Not to slack on my job, I stand from the stool to check on the kitchen staff. Hopefully, they're not swamped. I enter the kitchen and yell at Willis, the chef. "Yo Will! How's it going tonight? Need any help in here?"

"Hey boss man, no we're doing good. It hasn't picked up yet. You know once they get them drinks in 'em it'll start picking up."

"Let me know if you need any help tonight. Don't forget we got inventory tomorrow before open."

"Yes sir. I'll be here."

"Alright then." I head back to the bar to greet the guests and notice Curves and her friend are not at the table anymore. I look around but don't see her. When I make my way to the other side of the room, I notice her on the dancefloor. Thank God she didn't leave. I swear I felt a loss briefly. What the fuck is wrong with me!

She's gorgeous. A few men are eyeing her as she sways to the music with her eyes closed. Nervously, I walk up and tap her on the shoulder. She immediately opens her eyes. The surprised look on her face tells me I wasn't who she was expecting. She says nothing, but stares at me for what seems like forever. I lean closer to her ear and ask, "Mind if I join you?" She obliges.

We begin a slow sway to the music when I ask for her name. "It's Jayce, and yours?" Even her voice is beautiful. She feels good in my arms and her body pressed against mine is about to drive me crazy.

In an attempt to focus, I introduce myself and ask her if she's enjoying the night. "Yes, it's going good so far. I was having a nice little moment before you interrupted me though," she says. Oh shit, I hope I didn't fuck up her night. I'm being the exact guy I didn't want to be. I scratch my head stalling for time. Fix it Q!

I offer my best go-to solution of buying her another drink. She gratefully accepts. I take Jayce's hand and lead her to the bar. I notice no ring on her finger. So far so good.

I signal for Joni for another round. She would have turned me down by now if she had a man, right? We engage in light, flirty conversation, and I can't stop staring into her eyes. Her smile is gorgeous, her lips are gorgeous, her body is fucking gorgeous. If I wasn't at work, I would ask to kiss her right here at the bar. On that note, I should probably mention to her I own the bar. But before I can do that, Joni brings over our drinks. "Cheers?"

She says, "What are we drinking to Quinton?"

Fucking your fine ass, I think to myself. Instead, to her, I say, "Cheers to a good night." Jayce takes the shot and places the glass on the bar top. I take a few sips of my water. "Dance with me?" I say extending my hand.

She places her hand in mine. I lead her back to the dancefloor giving direct eye contact to any man looking my way. Letting them know she belongs to me. I need these other guys to back off. I spin her into my arms. Her ass rubbing against my dick has my blood rushing. She smells like vanilla and some expensive perfume. I slowly rub her body, needing to feel those curves in my hand. She abruptly turns around to face me to say she needs to use the restroom.

Did I move too fast? Did I mess it up? I watch her walk away. I start walking toward the bar. No, fuck that! I turn back around and head toward the restroom. I should at least apologize. I hope I didn't offend her or make her uncomfortable. She has me all out of my element, doing things I wouldn't normally do.

I strut down the hallway leading to the restrooms and wait until she exits in hopes she'll accept my apology. I lift my head to find her exiting the restroom. She approaches me with a smile, "What are you doing?"

She doesn't appear angry to see me. "I don't know to be honest. I'm just so drawn to you. Hoping I wasn't too forward earlier." I give it a moment to see if she says 'no.' My breathing is heavy with anticipation. The opposite happens. She leans in to kiss me and I reciprocate the kiss. My dick is jumping and struggling to break free against my jeans. Damn, I need to fuck badly. I passionately turn her around and press her against the wall. I then reach into her dress to palm her breasts which easily fill my hands with some to spare. I squeeze her nipples demanding them to harden under my touch. I place my other hand around her neck, stealing kisses while squeezing her nipple again and again. Her body melts into mine.

Reluctantly, I remove my hand from her dress after a guy exits the restroom. Jayce gives that same line again, "I should go check on my girl.”

I head into the men's restroom and try to release my bladder but to no avail. I stand there for a few minutes, looking in the mirror and cursing myself. Dammit Q, get it together. I wash my hands and splash some water on my face. Since I opened the bar, I've never behaved like this. Actually, it's been easy thus far to keep my personal and business life separate. She's the first woman that's made me lose my cool on the job.

We have some unfinished business. I exit the restroom and head straight towards her table. I immediately greet her friend in the red dress.

Red Dress introduces herself as Lydia. My mind is focused on Jayce, though.

“Jayce, can I talk to you for a minute?” Honestly, I have no idea what I want to talk about.

She follows me to my office. I usher her into the small space and close the door behind us. I take a seat behind the desk. I offer her a seat, but she remains standing.

“So, what did you need to talk about Quinton?”

“To be honest, I wanted to hear what more your body has to say. You keep running from me. No matter what comes out of your sexy little mouth. Your body says you want me.” Hoping this time alone could lead somewhere. I know she's more than just a quick fuck. I want to take her out and learn whatever she's willing to teach. At the same time, my body is begging for a release.

I try my best to communicate my feelings, then ask her what she wants, whether from me, from a relationship, or whatever. I just need to know. Jayce replies, “I’ve had a few too many shots to be sure of anything right now. It’s crazy that you seem so sure of whatever this is. Am I attracted and physically turned on by you? Yes. That’s not enough for me.”

So, she does want me. A smile creeps on my face. “Don’t just dismiss me. There’s something about you. I don’t want to spend the rest of my life thinking about Jayce, this woman I met at the bar once.” My own words surprise me. I could never talk with

Big Booty Tonya like this. Jayce is everything I didn't know I was looking for.

She tries to run again giving me that 'need to check on my homegirl' line again. What do I say to extend this time with her? I boldly call her over. "Come over here." I tap my lap for her to come and sit. There's a long quiet pause. She stares deep into my eyes. I feel maybe that wasn't the right thing to say.

Surprisingly, she strides over to me and begins pulling up her dress. I may have forgotten how to breathe, because she takes my breath away with her thick thighs and black lace panties. She removes her thong and I immediately stand to take her into my arms. I lean down and kiss her beautiful lips, grabbing her voluptuous bare ass, but what I really want to do is kiss those other lips. I'm trying to see how sweet she tastes. I need her pussy in mouth. "Bend over. Put your hands on the chair Jayce."

She doesn't hesitate to bend over. Look at that ass! If only she knew how bad I need this. I pull a condom from the desk drawer to let her know I have protection.

I kneel behind her. Eating pussy from the back is a fucking turn on. It's my go-to move. Plus, women seem to love that shit. I suckle on her clit and kiss her luscious lips. She whispers my name, providing more than enough motivation to proceed. I dart my tongue in and out her pussy. She's so fucking wet already I should just fuck her. Instead, I spread her cheeks. My mouth waters. I place my tongue in her ass just to hear her call out to me again. "Quinton, I'm about to cum." Blatantly ignoring her, I keep going until her ass shakes violently against my face and her body stops convulsing. Hearing her orgasm has me edging to the nth degree.

I stand to reach for the condom with one hand and lower my pants to release my dick from confinement with the other. Jayce turns around a takes my dick into her hand. She slowly licks upward against the head of my dick. I can clearly see the pre-cum on her tongue. Oh fuck! I'm not going to last much longer if she keeps doing this. With no hands, she sucks me into her mouth. I mean full suction like a fucking vacuum hose. She repeats again and again.

I need to feel some pussy though. I remove my dick from her mouth. I've asked a woman to stop before, but to literally pull my dick from her mouth is beautiful. I want to put it back in just to see it again. Lil big man jerks wildly as my release tries to escape me. I seek a reason to stall.

I look down at her. "You didn't follow my instructions Jayce. What did I tell you do?" I observe the puzzled look on her face for a moment. She's so damn sexy. "Stand up and bend over. Hands on the chair." I take off my shirt and open the condom. I roll it on while staring at her brown round ass. I witness her pussy juices dripping down to her clit.

I enter her. Fuck! This nut is going to come quick. Her walls are gripping me tight. I pull out and enter her again. She backs her ass up against me. Baby girl knows what she's doing. "Jayce," I say. I stroke her hard. "Give me your fucking number. I'm not stopping until you give me your number."

Her moaning is music to my ears. "Jayce, damn baby. Tell me you want me." The strokes pick up speed.

She finally says, "I'll give it to you. I promise." I grunt loudly as my body weakens. I cum hard and fast. I struggle to stand, stumbling wildly. She stands to offer me the chair. I sit, in a trance and breathing heavily.

Speechless, I watch her pick up her panties off the floor and grab her purse. "Don't leave," I try to say, but no words come out. Jayce grabs a pen from my desk and writes down her number.

"Here's my number."

"Good girl," is all I can manage to say at that moment.

She thanks me, and walks out of the office.

The door closes. In a panic, I reach for my phone and dial the number she left. Within a few seconds, she answers. With relief, I say, "Goodnight, Jayce."

Present Day . . .

With her elbow resting on the table, Jayce's hand covers her mouth. Her lifted eyebrows show the lines in her forehead. "Oh, my goodness! Yeah, that's a little different than how I saw it."

Danny says, "You didn't spare any details!" Danny leans back in his chair inhaling and exhaling a large breath of air.

"You guys make our story sound like child's play. We cannot be that boring, can we?" Chivon asks Danny. She sees the lustful look in his eyes.

Quinton is still closely observing the couple's conservative walls begin to fall. Danny's hand moves underneath the table, causing Chivon to shyly look away. Unlike the start of dinner, Chivon leans in closer to Danny with her arm hooked through his.

Quinton chuckles, "You can thank me later!"

Jayce laughs, "Don't be like that!"

Quinton shrugs his shoulders at Jayce. A smirk covers his face. "What?"

"You know what!" Jayce turns to Chivon. "He gets a thrill out going too far."

Quinton shakes his head, "Naw! That's not it. I just like love, and the sexual intimacy that goes along with it. It's beautiful and it makes people happy. Am I wrong? Just look at y'all!"

Danny and Chivon stare in each other eyes. "You might be on to something."

Jayce rubs Quinton's arm slowly. She whispers, "What if I didn't give you my number?"

Quinton turns to look in her eyes. "I don't know. I'm learning not to question fate." He smiles. "It brought me you!"

Undressed

Heavy rain pattering against the windows has me sluggish to rise this morning. The dark skies fooling my brain to assume the sun has not yet risen. Glancing at the clock, it reads 9:02 a.m. I lay there, staring at the ceiling, recalling my to-do list for the day: laundry, gym, and two piano instructions scheduled this afternoon.

Not to mention a potential gig tonight for our band. The band consists of Levi, Guy, Hindia, and myself. My name is Sidney, but most people call me Sid. I'm on the keyboard. Levy's our lead singer. We've got a hippie guitarist from Florida named Guy. And my closest friend, Hindia, both sings and plays the drums. We all met at a music retreat at Lake Tahoe three years ago. Our respective high schools provided a grant-funded program aimed at discovering musicians and artists. Instinctively, our paths collided at the retreat. After returning to Los Angeles, we kept in touch, and after a few jam sessions, we combined our gifts, which led to creating our band. The type of music we create is neo-soul and rock with a touch of R&B. The combination of our talents is an undiscovered treasure, hence our band name: *Grailway*.

The alarm clock sounds off loudly. "Ugh, I'm up already." I reach for my cell phone to dismiss the alarm. Exiting the bed, I stumble into the bathroom to release my bladder. After washing my hands, my face and brushing my teeth, I take my usual seat by the living area window. A loud beep aches my ears. The timer on the automatic coffee maker indicates the fresh brew is ready. Hurriedly, I grab a red coffee mug from the cabinet to pour a cup of dark roast, adding a dash of cream and two tablespoons of sugar. Lastly, I grab my music notebook and the cup of coffee before returning to the padded bench by the window.

Morning is my time of reflection and creativity. For some reason, songwriting flows more freely in the morning. Possibly, the mind is most clear before the happenings of the day take over. I sit by the window observing the locals and tourists strolling the streets of Playa del Rey.

Opening my notebook to read over the song I finished last night, I wonder if it still sounds as good as it did yesterday. Briefly, peering out of the window at the condo building across the street, I immediately notice the bathroom light turn on. My condo is on the 5th floor; his looks to be on the 4th floor of his building. He approaches the window and waves. I return a smile. I do not know his name, nor have I seen him outside of our buildings. Is it not strange, we live across the street from each other, but have never officially met?

His skin appears to be the color of cork oak. His teeth glow against his skin. He must be about six feet tall. His building is close enough to see him, but not close enough to read his facial expressions. I can't recall the exact day this little exchange began, but I thoroughly enjoy it.

The words in the notebook stare back at me. My mind is distracted. Intuitively, my head turns back to his window just as he takes off his pajama bottoms. With no underwear to remove, he stands naked, reaching for his toothbrush.

I inhale a huge breath of air in hopes of calming my libido. He's not a muscle-bound, beautiful god-like specimen of a man, more like an average forty-year-old guy. It could be the dick drought I'm currently experiencing or only having sex once since breaking up with my ex-boyfriend four months ago. The attention sure is flattering.

Nearly a month ago, during my morning routine, I looked out of the window at nothing in particular. Lost in my thoughts, I didn't notice him watching me but somehow, he caught my eye. He smiled and waved, so I offered the same in return. Deliberately, he removed his clothes, knowing I watched. Completely caught off guard, I gathered my coffee and notebook to exit his line of sight. A week later, it happened again. I casually looked over at his window. To my surprise, the naked guy across the street is in the shower looking directly at me. Before I could turn away, he began stroking his dick. I quickly turned away in shock from his bold actions, but curiosity got the best of me, so my eyes revert toward the window again. He watched me, watch him jerk off. I pondered if I am the creep for watching or if he is creepy for wanting me to see. His sexual, carefree nature turned me on. He was in his own space, without a care, releasing his frustration to start his day.

That is the backstory of how this peek-and-see game began. Now here I am preparing for another morning of meditation. I shamelessly watch him stroke himself while letting the water fall over his face. His mouth slightly parts as he catches a rhythm. My pussy aches watching him pleasure himself, prompting me to reach into my panties to rub my swelling clit. It grows more sensitive with each touch. My middle finger slips inside my wet pussy, stroking to match his rhythm. A buzzing sound breaks my concentration. I look down to find my phone buzzing against the window seal. Who is interrupting this captivating moment? It's a text message from Guy.

The band group text reads:

Guy: On for tonight. 8pm @ WatchHouse. We open up. Be on time.
Hindia: sid, can you pick me up?
 Me: Awesome! Good looking out Guy. Hindi I can pick u up.
Levi: Cool. About 2 b crazy night
 Hindia: art fest always bring out crazies LOL. see u tonight

Finally, peering up from my phone, the guy across the street is exiting the shower with a towel around his waist. Nonchalantly I shrug my shoulders to say, "Guess it's not my day."

Undressed – Ch. 2

The day drifted by quicker than expected. The piano instructions didn't end until nearly six this evening, leaving just enough time to hurry home, shower and dress for the show tonight. I check the fit of my black tank top and black jeans in the mirror. I fluff my big afro with my hands. Slipping on my platform boots and grabbing my purse, I lock the door. In the car, I text Hindia I'll arrive in twenty minutes.

In comparison to a usual Friday night in Los Angeles, the traffic is light on the I-110 North towards the University of Southern California. I'm steadily on route to Hindia's place. The twenty-five-minute drive could have easily been over an hour commute on a normal traffic day. I pull up to Hindia's apartment building and blow the horn. A few minutes later, she lugs her equipment down the stairs. Her long, dark Indian hair is pulled into a messy bun. She wears a black mini dress and black boots. I open the hatch and hop out the driver's side to help her load the SUV.

"Hey girl! How've you been?" I ask.

"Hey there. It's been hectic with classes and my parents. Other than that, it's good. We haven't had a gig in like a month, right?"

"Yes, it feels like forever." We embrace in a quick hug. "Come on, let's get downtown before Guy starts blowing up our phones. Do not need him in his feelings tonight."

Hindi replies, "You know how he feels about you. He's been liking you since like forever."

We share a laugh before driving off. I don't want to get into a long conversation my him right now.

"You all barely made it!" Levi yells at us as we approach the stage. Levi's sandy brown curls hang to his shoulders. We all exchange hugs and laughs like we haven't seen each other in years.

Guy states, "They moved the time out like 20 mins. Everything else is ready. Just waiting on you guys. We have about 15 minutes to finish setting up and sound check." He pauses to look down at his phone. "Levi, did you update social media yet?" His demeanor serious and unwavering.

"No, about to do it now. Let me finish helping the girls with the equipment," says Levi.

Hindia and Levi exit the stage, leaving Guy and I alone. I try to gauge his mood, but the minimal lighting hides his dark eyes. He asks, "What's up? You doing okay?"

"Hey Guy. You excited about tonight?"

He steps in closer and whispers, "So, you're going to act like nothing happened between us?"

We had a night of fun last month after our last gig. It was a weak moment and I regretted it the moment we were done. We're good just as friends. His long hair and tanned skin prove him attractive to many women, but I don't want to mess up the chemistry we have as a band. I try to spare his feelings. "Guy, we had sex once. We were drunk and had a fun night. That's all."

Through saving grace, the bar manager signals a thumbs-up, saving me from this awkward conversation. We take our places on stage. Hindi and Levi check the microphone volumes. Levi taps the mic and introduces the band to the crowd. The crowd is larger than expected, especially with us being the first band to perform. Forty or fifty people will hear us play tonight, possibly tripling once the main act performs. This could be a good night for us!

Levi taps his foot heavily against the floor. "Let's go. One, two, three…"

The bar allowed extra set time after the next band didn't show up. The crowd loved it! We played mostly original songs and a few classic neo-soul covers for nearly thirty-five minutes, making it the longest set we've ever played.

We exit the stage gathering our gear and equipment. In the parking lot, we high five and congratulate each other. The adrenaline high vibrates through my body. "OMG, that was so much fun!" I excitedly mention to Guy.

"Agreed. That was one of the best sets we've had so far. Did you see all the people dancing?"

"Yeah, I knew they'd love your song. 'Lose Me' always gets people out of their seats."

There's a tap on my shoulder. "Pardon me." I look up from packing the equipment to see Guy looking behind me. I turn around to see what captured his attention, finding a good-looking man I've never met. His beautiful light brown skin and dreadlocks catch my eye, a small hoop ring pierces his nose and thick right eyebrow. He resembles Lenny Kravitz, with a smooth heavy accented voice like Idris Elba.

He says, "I loved the show. Your band is really good."

"Thank you! Glad you enjoyed it. You have an accent. Where are you from?"

"I'm from London, but I just recently relocated here for work. Oh, my name is Jon, by the way. May I ask your name?" He extends his hand to me.

"It's Sidney, but everyone calls me Sid," my hand reaching out to shake his.

"Sidney, I tried to gain your attention earlier. If not too forward, would you like to go out sometime? It would be great to make new friends here."

Straight to the point and completely caught me off guard. I look at him inquisitively. "Umm, I'm not sure, Jon. I'm not really looking for new friends."

Hindia yells over the loud chatter of the crowd. "Sid, you almost ready?"

"Come on Sidney! We can exchange information and see where it goes from there." His smile brightens the room. Why does he have to be so cute?

"I'm coming Hindi."

I bat my eyes at Jon and hold out my hand. "Give me your phone."

Jon removes his phone from his pocket, unlocks it and places it in my hand. I enter my name and number before handing it back to him.

"Thank you. We will talk soon. Have a fair night, Sidney!"

With a smile, I respond, "Goodnight, Jon."

Undressed - Ch. 3

After leaving WatchHouse, we decide to visit our favorite downtown bar, Hugo's, for post-show drinks. We recapped the night's events and brainstormed new ideas for our next gig. My thoughts wander back to the cute guy, Jon, at WatchHouse. His demeanor was cool and laid back. I wonder what part of the city he's staying in? What does he do for work? What is he like in bed?

In an attempt to disconnect from my thoughts, I ask Hindi if she's ready to call it a night. It's nearing midnight when we finally exit Hugo's and say our goodbyes to Guy and Levi.

"It was a good night, no?" Hindi asks on the drive back to her place.

"I had fun. Think we'll have another gig soon after tonight! That place loved us."

"I think so too! Thanks again for the ride. I'll call you later this week so we can collab on that new song you were talking about. Ooh, we can meet up for lunch or something!"

I pull up to her building. "We can finally try that Ethiopian spot in Inglewood we've been talking about!"

We've talked about visiting the restaurant for the past year. Hindia exits the passenger door. "Yes, let's do that! Night girl. Get home safe." She removes her equipment from the trunk and makes her way up the stairs to her apartment.

"Goodnight!" I yell after her.

The ride home is quiet. No music, just my thoughts. Jon is still on my mind. I hope he calls because he could be my new fuck buddy. His woodsy masculine scent still lingers in my senses.

I click the garage opener on my key chain and the automatic gate to the condo's parking garage opens. I park my SUV and grab my keyboard from the trunk. My tired body drags through the hallway onto the elevator. A shower and sleep are the only activities on my agenda tonight.

At my door, a folded piece of paper sticks out from the doorframe. I look down the hallway as if someone will appear. Placing my key in the door, I hurriedly snatch the note and enter the apartment, locking both locks after me. I open the folded paper. The note reads:

Let's stop playing this little game. Come over. - #412

The guy from across the street has boldly made a move. Does he expect me to just show up at his place? Who does he think I am! His words replay in my mind over again as I shower. I try to let the irritation wash over me as I contemplate what would happen if I did or did not go to his place. Will he stroke me as smoothly as he strokes himself?

My brain is leading my body into dangerous territory. I choose a cute pair of panties to wear to bed. Next, I find myself checking myself in the mirror. Who am I kidding? Playing one round wouldn't hurt, right?

"What am I doing?" I exhale heavily before knocking on the door. There's silence on the other side of the door. I contemplate walking away, feeling both foolish and daring. Suddenly, footsteps approach the door. I lower my head in hopes he doesn't see the shame on my face.

The door opens. "Didn't think you would come?"

I look up at him and try not to gasp aloud. What the hell? Turns out he's not that cute at all and not my usual type. He has a decent body, but I can't quite recall who or what he resembles.

"Yeah, I got your note."

"You want to come in?" He opens the door wide, welcoming me to enter.

Still unsure, I glare at him again in hopes to recognize his uncanny appearance. "Umm, sure. But only for a little bit. I've had a long day." Upon entry, my eyes scan the living space of his condo. The décor is stunning. "Did you hire someone to decorate? Your place is really nice!"

He closes the door and follows me into the living area. "Sort of. My ex owed me a favor. I helped him out with starting his own interior design business a few years ago. This was his way of repaying me. Hey, what's your name?"

"It's Sid, and yours?"

"Miles. Nice to finally meet you. Want something to drink? Water, wine, beer."

Instead of taking a seat on the couch, I follow him to the kitchen. "White wine is fine."

"Did I hear you correctly? You said your ex was a guy?" I attempt to read his facial expressions.

He smiles. Pouring the wine, he responds, "Yes, we dated about a year. Is that a problem?"

I cough to clear my throat. "No, I just didn't expect it, that's all. So, what do you do Miles? From all the high-tech gadgets in here, it has to be something in IT."

"Good detective work, Sid." He circles the large kitchen island. "Here's your wine. You smoke? I can roll up if you want."

I take a sip of wine. "No, thanks. The wine is enough. This is really good wine by the way!"

I follow him to the living area. We take a seat on the huge white L-shaped sectional sofa. "Thank you. It's a 2013 Chardonnay from a local vineyard in Napa owned by a close friend. I'm curious, why do you sit in the window every morning? I thought you were just being nosy initially, but I noticed you were always reading something."

After a few more sips of wine, I reply. "I write music. That's my usual time to write and clear my head. I was so shocked that day you undressed, knowing that I saw you. Once you went further, I just, couldn't stop watching."

He bites down on his bottom lip. "To be honest, it wasn't planned. I was turned on just knowing you were watching. You could have easily turned away, but you didn't. Now here we are." He looks at me intently, "What were you hoping would happen coming over tonight?"

Contemplating his question. I shamelessly state, "An orgasm."

He responds by smiling and nodding his head. Miles stands and removes the wine glass from my hand, placing it on the table. I grudgingly stare at the cold glass of amazing wine missing from hand. He extends his hand. "Come with me." Cautiously, I take his hand as he guides me into his spacious bedroom. Miles sits at the foot of the platform bed. "Undress for me Sid."

The lighting is low, but I still see his less than attractive face. I close my eyes and imagine the orgasm I desperately need. "Really? You want to watch me undress?"

With confidence, he replies, "You asked for an orgasm, right? I can do that for you, but I need you to do this for me."

I guess I'll have to remove my clothes anyway if I want that orgasm. I slowly remove my flip flop sandals, taking my time pulling the USC t-shirt over my head.

He says, "Come closer."

After few steps forward, I remove my yellow gym shorts. His eyes linger over my half-naked body in only a bra and panties. His erection is visibly noticeable under his pajama bottoms. My body is heating up fast, with no hesitation of turning back. I remove my bra and pull down my panties, letting them fall to the floor.

Strutting over to Miles, I place my goodies in his face. "Touch me."

His hands ease up the back of my slim thighs up to my small tight ass. He falls back on the bed, pulling me on top of him. "Climb up here Sid. Let me taste you."

The words sound like music to my ears. I crawl up his body until my ass covers his face. He immediately plants his face deep into my pussy, entering me roughly with his tongue.

"Oh!" My body shivers from his touch. Damn, he's professional! He darts his tongue in and out my pussy. Then, he slides his tongue between my pussy lips, lightly rubbing against my clit. My moans fill the room. "Again, please. Yes, again."

He does as instructed. The wet sounds from him lapping his tongue between my fold nearly sends me into overdrive. Just as I find a steady pace. He stops to suck on my lips. His warm mouth covering my pussy is a blissful feeling. I'm getting so close. I grind my clit against his tongue and I ride his face hard.

The image of Jon, the cute guy from the bar, pops into my head. I imagine Jon's tongue licking my pussy. His hands massaging my breasts. "Oooh, don't stop." Within seconds, my body tenses and a euphoric sensation invades my senses with the most intense orgasm I've ever felt. Whimpers escape my lips with every contraction of my walls.

I roll my body off of his face onto the pillows. He sits up on the bed. Satisfied with his work, he asks. "How was that?"

No words escape me. I lay there sedated in all my naked glory, unable to utter a word. His hands massage my thighs. "Sid, say you want more? Let me give you more."

With what little strength I have, I lift up on my elbows. I look into his eyes. The after-nut clarity is a real thing. I finally figured it out.

He looks like a damn armadillo! I smile, trying not to laugh out loud. "Do you have protection, Jon?"

His body jolting on his feet. "What did you say?" He crinkles his nose.

"I asked did you have protection?" I know he heard me.

"No, you called me Jon. Come on, that's not cool. For real?" He shakes his head in disbelief. "Did you really just call me some other dude's name?"

"You should go." His voice is stern. He seems more agitated than angry.

"Sorry, Miles. I didn't mean to. It just slipped out." Wow, he actually bought it! Surprised the intentional name slip worked, I offer my best 'I'm so sorry face' while putting on my clothes. He stands there silently, waiting for me to gather my things.

He hurries me to the door. "I'm so sorry. Hope you have a good night, Miles." I say exiting his condo. I have a feeling I may have fucked up a guaranteed orgasm for a cute face, but I immediately think back to his armadillo features. Nope, not gonna be able to do it!

I look down at my phone. There's a new message.

Jon: *It was nice meeting you. Hope to see you soon.*

A huge smile covers my face on the short walk home. "Guess this is my day after all."

The First Date

Branden knocks on Ashleigh's apartment door, intentionally arriving early for respectable rapport. During his years playing college football, his coach always pressed it's better to be early than on time. Now, Branden is thankful for heeding such wise advice.

Ashleigh peeks nervously through the peephole. She opens the door and greets Branden with a warm smile. Her sight is immediately drawn to his dark brown eyes and how they crease in the corners when he smiles. The freshly lined beard hides his thin lips.

"Hi. You look as beautiful as I remember," he stares. Her cat-like eyes, full lips, and curvy slim physique entice him just the same as two weeks ago.

Ashleigh's senses heighten when they embrace in a hug. She inhales his masculine cologne mixed with a faint scent of marijuana. He, too, looks better than she remembered. Branden is dressed to impress, wearing a casual mustard-colored sweater that highlights his brown skin. The casual black business pant is fitted to show a bulge the left of his zipper. A stylish brown hat and brown boots complete his expression of European fashion.

"Want to come in?" Ashleigh asks.

His eyes skim over Ashleigh when she turns around, welcoming him to follow her inside. Her natural hair is straightened down her back, bringing attention to her thin waist and tight ass. The flowy, short, cobalt blue skirt and white, long sleeve, off-the-shoulder top compliments her dark skin tone. The gold jewelry glows against her skin; she's styled effortlessly like an African goddess.

Ashleigh attempts to regain Branden's attention. "Branden. Branden."

"My bad. Damn, you look so good." He looks her up and down. "You clean up nice," he jokes.

She snickers at his observation. "So do you."

Unlike their initial encounter, there's a noticeable change in appearance. Two weeks ago, hiking at Runyon Canyon, Branden and his younger brother stopped to capture the city view. He noticed a group of women posing and taking pictures. He and Ashleigh locked eyes at the same time. Branden almost continued on with his hike, but conscious energy pushed him to say hello. Feeling like a shy schoolgirl, Ashleigh and her friends giggled bashfully as he approached. He extended his hand to introduce himself to Ashleigh. She accepted the handshake and told him her name.

Witnessing her up-close allowed Branden to see the plump breasts and perky ass hiding under Ashleigh's workout clothes. He complimented her beauty and eagerly asked for her number. Ashleigh was shocked. She didn't see herself in the portrait he described. She didn't have on any makeup, and her hair was a frizzy mess. She didn't feel the same beauty his eyes painted. However, in her eyes, he looked incredibly sexy in a cut-off shirt, covered in sweat. His muscular legs glistening in the sun. Branden dialed her number into his phone, and after a few more pleasantries, they parted ways.

Branden called her later that night, surprising Ashleigh by calling so soon. He didn't adhere to the normal 'wait a day' dating standards society created. They talked and texted for hours nearly every day since. The following week, Ashleigh traveled to Mexico for a planned girl's trip. Unfortunately, between the trip, conflicting work schedules, and obligatory social engagements, they couldn't find time to meet up over those two weeks. They unknowingly allowed anticipation to nurture their mental and emotional connection, that may someday collide with the physical attraction.

Ashleigh asks, "You ready to go? I just need to put on my boots."

Branden no longer cares to go out. He purchased tickets to the fall music festival held at Griffith Park. He would prefer to spend his time learning Ashleigh's body. "Wait," he blurts.

"Wait? What for?" Ashleigh stands before him, not sure of what he's asking. She attempts to read his body language.

A mischievous look fills his eyes. Branden replies. "Don't put on your boots yet. Can you remove the stockings?"

"You don't like them? The weather is cool today; I didn't want my ass to freeze." She looks down at her legs. Her arms bent with her hands facing upward. Confusion is written over her face. Ashleigh ponders if he's controlling, prompting him to critique her on the first date. Or is he just highly interested in fashion?

Branden notices a change in her demeanor. The cute, flirty attitude she just once possessed is fading. She seems bothered. "No! No, beautiful. I like the flesh-toned stockings." Branden sticks his hands in pocket. "But honestly, I'll probably want to fuck you at some point today. Those might get in my way." He nervously flirts with the intention of reviving her lively attitude.

Ashleigh's eye contact is direct. A smile creeps on her face. She's blushing, triggering heat to flush her skin. Her body temperature rising faster than she can process the change. Unconsciously, she waves her hand to cool her face.

He chuckles. "Am I making you hot?" The innocence covering her face tempts him to want her more, although he knows it's a front. After their deep conversations, he knows her level of sexual experience is higher than she's leading on right now.

Branden inches closer to her. "Let me help you."

His hands wrap around her waist. He holds her tight. The feel of her body compliments him perfectly. Branden leans in to kiss her, allowing her time to reciprocate. Her arms slowly raise, landing on his shoulders. Her hands rub the back of his head. The kiss quickly igniting passion between them. Ashleigh allows Branden's hands to linger over her body. He reaches under her skirt. Ashleigh breaks the kiss to look Branden in his eyes. She silently provides permission to continue. He proceeds by pulling the stockings over her hips. He slowly bends down on one knee, removing the stockings from each leg. Her smooth, soft bare legs beg his attention. Ashleigh's breathing grows ragged when he runs his hands up her legs. Her pussy is moist from his lustful gazes, but grows wetter with every touch. She boldly lowers her thong over her hips. Branden acknowledges her consent by covering his hands with hers, finishing the removal of her panties.

She leads him over to the sofa and sits, then leans back on the armrest while Branden kneels in front of her. He lowers his head, licking his lips at the sight of her freshly shaven pussy. He readily dives in, sucking both pussy lips into his mouth. Ashleigh's head falls back, moaning at his vigor to taste her. "Umm. Uh. Umm."

Branden spreads her lips, nibbling gently on her bud; he rotates, biting and licking, licking and sucking. Ashleigh admires his talent to please. Her body shifting beneath him, moving to catch a rhythm. Branden bends her legs, folding her body in half. Her fat pussy tempting him to fuck her raw. Settling on his second-best option, his mouth covers her pussy, darting his tongue between her fold. Suddenly, Branden stops. A look of disappointment spreads across Ashleigh's face. Ashleigh's eyes snap open to witness the reason he abruptly stopped eating her pussy. She smiles when she sees Branden remove a condom from his back pocket.

"You came prepared, didn't you?" Ashleigh asks.

No longer wasting time to be inside her, he unbuttons his pants, pulling them down to expose his full erection. Ashleigh watches him with excitement. The size of his dick is bigger than she expected. Branden opens the condom and covers himself. He pulls Ashleigh down to the floor. He turns her around on her knees, she rests her upper body against the sofa cushions. "Yes!" she exclaims when he enters her in a single stroke.

Branden fucks her hard. He attempts to slow down, but the constriction of her walls clenches him. He couldn't escape if he wanted to. Ashleigh rocks her hips, backing her ass against him and meeting his strokes halfway. Branden grips her waist and pumps her fast. Ashleigh fucks him back, matching his rhythm. Unable to control his orgasm, he pulls out and convulses against her back, filling the condom with his semen. His heavy breathing echoes throughout the room. Branden and Ashleigh sit contently sedated, smiling, unsure how they ended up half naked on the floor.

The late afternoon Los Angeles weather is beautiful. The warm sun providing the perfect amount of heat to balance the cool fall breeze. Before arriving at the music festival, Branden and Ashleigh shopped for snacks and drinks at a nearby grocery store. After their midday quickie, they easily settle into physical comfortability by holding hands and kissing while shopping. They purchased a small cooler, ice, a twist cap bottle of wine, beer, cheese, crackers, prepared fresh-cut fruit, and potato chips. Branden borrowed two lawn chairs from his father for him and Ashleigh to sit in the park.

Branden's SUV pulls into the parking lot of Griffith Park. His hand rests on Ashleigh's thigh. The city park is jam-packed with music fans and families seeking a relaxing daytime fun-filled activity. Once they finally park, Ashleigh leans over to kiss Branden. Before he could open the driver's door, she starts feeling him up by rubbing his thigh. He attempts to stop her, "Come on. We already...", but she eagerly cuts him off with another kiss. Her tongue searching his mouth, tasting herself on his tongue. Branden adjusts the driver's seat back as far as it will go. Ashleigh steps over the middle console and sits in his lap, the horn blowing as she finds a comfortable position.

"Open the glove compartment," Branden says while partially pulling down his pants to release his erection. Ashleigh reaches over to open the compartment. A three-pack box of condoms nearly falls to the passenger floor. She peeks into the open box, noticing two condoms remain. She removes one and hands it to him. Ashleigh lifts herself to raise her skirt, also pulling her thong to the side, while he rolls on the condom to responsibly protect them.

"Come here." He tugs down on her waist. Ashleigh accepts his wrapped gift by easing down, guiding his dick inside her still wet pussy. Grateful the dark tint on his SUV hides them from public eyes, she grinds her clit back and forth against him, seeking the orgasm she lost earlier. Her moans loudly fill the confined space of the car. Branden lifts her skirt to witness her ass grinding against him. He grips her ass hard with both hands. Branden licks his lips wishing he could bite a piece of her sweetness.

Branden wants her to achieve the orgasm he was too impatient to provide her earlier. His hands roam underneath her top, into her strapless bra to fondle her perfectly round breasts. "Yes! Please yes!" Ashleigh screams.

His erection grows harder hearing her moans. Branden pinches her small nipples between his fingers. He bites his bottom lip, wishing they were in his mouth instead. Ashleigh's moans reach a new height. The moans grow louder as she continues working her hips against him. "Umm! Hmm!" Ashleigh tightly closes her eyes shut. Her pussy contracts, gripping him tight as her orgasm arises. "Shit, I'm about to cum. Branden!" Her body becomes rigid as she releases. She grabs the steering wheel to steady herself from slumping over onto the dash.

Branden allows a few moments for Ashleigh's body to settle before he grips her ass, lifting her up and down on his dick. His hips thrust upward as she bounces. His strokes became faster and harder. Ashleigh spits in her hand and reaches between her legs to fondle his balls, never losing her rhythm riding his dick. He groans loudly. With short and hard pumps, he fucks her until his body tingles, signifying his orgasm has arrived.

With one last thrust in her wet pussy, he growls and releases without pulling out. "Grrr!" Roaring like a wild animal in the jungle. His weak body collapses deep into the bucket seat; their heavy breathing fogs the windows. Ashleigh climbs back over the middle console, tumbling on the passenger seat.

The sit quietly, neither of them can figure out how this happened again. Branden pulls up his pants, thinking of a way to dispose of the condom. As if reading his mind, Ashleigh passes him a few napkins from the open glove compartment. "Here."

"Thank you. How you know?" he asks teasingly.

"You're not that hard to read," she states matter-of-factly.

"Whatever," he chuckles. "Come on. Let's see if we can still find a good spot to sit."

"Did you have a good time? I mean the way you were dancing all night! I would say you did," Branden asks. After a couple of drinks, they slow danced and rocked out to the music. They also fed each other fruit and cheese, enjoying the time with each other.

Ashleigh replies, "I had a great time. This has to be the best first date!" She staggers slightly as they return to the car. She let loose after a couple of cups of wine, from dancing to the different performing artists to conversing with the other festival-goers. Branden couldn't help the growing attraction to her. Her free spirit captured his heart. He witnessed nearly the full realm of her in just a few hours, which he never did with his ex-girl-friend. They dated two years, and he knew nothing about her.

"Yea. This day has been on another level." He leans in to kiss her. "To your place?" Branden asks helping her into the car.

"Yes, please!" He closes her door and enters on the driver's side.

Branden exits the parking lot and navigates the streets back to her apartment off the Sunset Strip. The light conversation suddenly takes a turn when Ashleigh asks Branden a simple question.

"Branden, what does making love feel like? I like sex! You seem to, too. But I can't say I've ever made love," Ashleigh admits. She's imagined it many times before but has never been fortunate enough to experience it for herself, only sex and fucking. She knows her young age of twenty-four may contribute to that missing aspect of her sex life.

"Have you been in love?" Branden asks.

"I don't know. I was infatuated with my ex mostly. When I think back on it, that couldn't have been love. And what sucks most is I'm a hopeless romantic!" She recalls the relationship with her verbally abusive ex-boyfriend. He was everything a woman thinks they want, yet lacked essential emotional maturity. As a result, what she thought was love, was nothing more than infatuation.

Branden glances over at Ashleigh. He rubs her thigh to calm her apparent uneasiness. "So, he never took his time to love you in bed."

"We had the usual lazy or early morning sex… You didn't answer my question, though! What does it feel like?"

Branden recalls his personal experiences and imagines how he would make love to Ashleigh. His lips twisted to one side of his face. Thoughtfully, he contemplates her question, taking his time to prepare a just response.

"Well… to me, making love feels like bliss… It's like your mind, your body, and soul are all happy at the same exact time." He pauses. "The moment is filled with this kind of overwhelming joy. Like nothing really matters except giving and pleasing and being vulnerable enough to receive." Branden pauses again, seeking words to accurately describe his thoughts. With tension in his eyes, he continues, "Your heart aches and craves. Aches so good that you want to cry. My god, the pussy gets so wet you don't want to pull out! I swear!" He shakes his head to exaggerate his point.

All Ashleigh could manage to say is, "Hmph!" She shifts in her seat picturing his lively words. The thought of such a euphoric experience stirs up a craving for more of him.

Branden follows up, "Of course, both people have to be on the same page. It's not making love if one person's mind or body not there. You know?"

"You are making me so horny right now. You have no idea." Ashleigh glares out the window, watching the street lights pass in a blur.

He observes her, sensing dejection from her. "Your mind is wandering. What you thinking about?" he says, reaching for her hand.

Ashleigh looks over at Branden. A second of silence lingers between them. Her grateful heart singing his melody and her voice barely above a whisper, she simply responds, "You."

Branden smiles and lifts her hand to his lips. He makes a right onto her street. "Everything I said. I want to do that with you. For you."

She gives an assuring smile, "I know!"

"You know, huh?" Branden pulls over in front of her building and parks the car.

Ashleigh retorts, "I mean, you do have one condom left. You know this could be a personal record. I've never had sex three times in one day!"

"It hasn't been a full day. Don't count me out. I'm just saying. You gonna owe me props after I get you out of those clothes though," Branden chuckles. "For real, this might just be your last first date."

Boots

F inally, she arrives. I slide the large steel door open. "Boots, I'm so sorry. I had a family—"

"You're late," I snarl in her face. "Tardiness is not acceptable. Face the door until I tell you to move."

"But Boots, I—"

"You know my rules, Bunny. Don't move. Don't talk. Do nothing until I say so." She does this every session, arriving later or earlier than the scheduled time. At this point, I'm certain she does it on purpose.

While she contemplates her disrespectful behavior, I'll give the backstory behind the name Boots. It was a nickname given to me by my NYU college roommate, Christian Brady. One Friday night at a bar, CB and I invited a few girls back to our apartment for drinks. We were having a fun night, playing drinking games and getting high. I started making out with one of the girls. Another girl started rubbing on me. One thing led to another, and we were all naked, having a good time. I was fucking one girl so hard that I slipped. Damn near busted my face on the hardwood floors. I knew I had to create a distraction from that embarrassing moment. Because of this, I put my Timberland boots on and knocked down all three girls. The next day me and CB, we laughed and reminisced on the night, which led to the nickname 'Boots.' I never lived that night down on campus. I used it to my advantage. Wearing the boots during sex just became a legend of its own. Many of the girls on campus wanted to fuck, just to witness it for themselves.

If it isn't obvious, let me explain what it is I do. I rented out a loft space just for fun nearly nine months ago. Initially, I would invite a friend or two over for some fun. We would have kinky sex-filled nights, usually with me dominating the room. That led to a few women asking for one-on-one time. They enjoyed being submissive, and I enjoyed taking advantage. It then dawned on me to charge a fee for my time. I saw no reason to throw away a good business idea, so I created a business plan. That's when Just Boots, LLC was born. The name is discreet on purpose, obviously. Many women feel the need to hide their expenses and spending habits. Having 'Boots' on a credit card statement lessens the suspicions and red flags from their spouse or partner.

The clientele applying for my services complete a sexual desires checklist. They check the boxes of the activities they've already experienced, what they would like to experience, and experiences that are completely off-limits. Bunny didn't hold back. She checked nearly every box. I modified the form to include an 'All of the Above' option because of her.

Don't get me wrong. This is a dangerous job. You would be surprised how many women show up without warning. Drunk women constantly show up horny, looking to get fucked. A few months ago, a girl broke the glass on the entrance door, all because I wouldn't buzz her up. After that night, it was clear I had to take this more seriously. I hired a security guard to man the entrance and lobby the following day.

I never asked Bunny how she learned about me or my services. There's no marketing budget, so I assume it was word of mouth from another client. Bunny isn't her legal name. It would be difficult to call her anything else at this point. During her first session, I ordered her to hop on my dick like a rabbit. On some freaky shit, it was an off the cuff thought and a rabbit was the first thing that came to mind. Without hesitation, she hopped on and rode me like an energized bunny. Ever since then, she's been my Bunny.

It's not feasible to get close with clients, for my own protection, of course. The less I know about their personal lives, the easier it is to do my job. However, Bunny has scheduled sessions for nearly the past five or six months. She faithfully schedules a monthly appointment. Honestly, most women don't last that long. They either fulfill a fantasy in a one-time experience or are too damn scared to return.

Curiosity got the best of me with Bunny. We smoked a little medicinal herb together after one session. I learned she's married with a kid and a lawyer at some big firm downtown. None of that makes a person though. If you stripped all that away, she would still be a sexual deviant. Bunny is beautiful. She is damn near perfect aesthetically. Brown skin, tall, wide hips, and a round ass. Not just her body, but her willingness to explore is extremely attractive.

Boots – Ch. 2

The loft is pitch black, illuminated only with green light and two red exit signs. The loft is spotless with a freshly washed comforter and silk sheets, thanks to the cleaning ladies. They faithfully change the linens and clean the space every morning. Except on Sunday and Monday when we're closed. Those are statistically slow business days for me because most women are usually busy taking care of their husbands and children, getting ready for the upcoming work week.

Suitably in my briefs and boots, I take a seat in my custom Head Master chair to watch her from across the room. The chair is located in the middle of the room on a five-inch-high circle platform. It's a high-back chair upholstered in green velvet. Bunny still stands with her eyes on the door. She shifts her weight from left to right. The shadow from her tall curvy frame is projected against the wall. "Move again and I will double your punishment."

Still seated, I demand, "Bunny, take off your clothes."

First, Bunny unbuttons and removes her blouse. I witness her curves from behind. She begins to turn around. "Did I say turn around? I specifically said take off your clothes. You don't fuckin listen." I pause, then bark at her, "Tonight, will not go well for you!" She quickly snaps her head back around and unzips her pencil skirt, letting it fall around her ankles.

Frustrated, I stand from my chair to walk over to her. My boots loudly thump against the concrete floors. Just as she removes her bra, I grab her neck from behind. "Why are you so disobedient today?" I remove the green bandana from the waistband of my briefs. I fold it and tie it over her eyes. In only her heels and thong, I guide her across the loft to the black king size poster bed.

I bend her over the foot of the bed, pushing her head down into the comforter. "I should put my boot up your ass for wasting my time. I don't want to hear a word from you tonight. Do you understand?"

"Yes, Boots!"

I smack her ass, "I said not a word."

Her whimpers are muffled through the sheets.

"Stretch out your arms." I extend her right arm, handcuff her wrist to the bedpost, and then do the same to her left wrist. She appears to have it all in life, but something must be really bad at home. If she could schedule more than once a month, she would probably be here every week. To build suspense, I don't allow clients to book more than once a month. It's best to keep it professional and not allow familiarity to breed entitlement. This isn't the type of business where the customer is always right. Not at Just Boots.

She's purposefully blindfolded because she has no idea what is about to go down tonight. What I like about Bunny is she never complains. Even if she did, she has already signed a non-disclosure agreement and a form of consent. No matter what I do to her, whips, chains, hot wax, etc., she has become one of my best test subjects. I get to fulfill my personal fantasies and kinks with her. Her husband must be an asshole or a complete square because Bunny is a freak. I mean, like a *real* freak. He must not know how to handle her, or she wouldn't need to be here with me.

For instance, last month, I put her in the sex swing. I fucked her hard. She kept asking for more. I damn near tapped out. That's not how this works. A big no-no in my book. I refuse to let that happen again. In this session, I'm determined to take back my power. She needs to know who's in charge.

Boots - Ch. 3

The loft's entryway wall has mounted shelving stocked with lubricants, condoms, and sex toys. "This will do." I grab a bottle of lubricant and a couple of sex toys from the shelf. My heavy boots leading the way, I make my way back towards the bed. Those long legs in heels, ass up and chained to the bed, are a sight to see. She is sexy as hell.

I smack her ass again. Obediently, she buries her head into the pillow to muffle her cries. The mesh white thong against her caramel-colored skin is stunning. Her cocoa scent lingers in the air. I snatch the thong from her tight desirable ass down to her ankles.

"I'm not taking it easy on you tonight, Bunny. You've pissed me off. Your punishment starts now." I remove the sex toy from the box, placing the J-shaped vibrator over her pussy and strapping it around her thighs. It almost looks like a slingshot. The small hook of the 'J' barely breaks the opening of the vagina. I turn the setting on low and watch her squirm and grind her hips against the bed. I'll wait until she subjects herself to cumming, but she's toying with me though. It's evident she is taking her time reaching an orgasm. I know what she likes, and I know her body. Why she chooses the hard way, I don't know.

After a few minutes, her body quivers and relaxes against the mattress. Her cries of pleasure ringing out are music to my ears. I drop my briefs, stepping out of them without removing my boots. I slowly approach her, dropping my heavy dick on her ass. "You don't deserve this dick."

I squeeze a small amount of lube on her left ass cheek, smearing it up and down the crack of her ass with my dick. I then take the two medium-sized anal balls and gradually place them into her tight little asshole. Dammit Bunny! My dick jumps as I watch her take it with ease. How does she so easily take me out of my element?

Before returning to the Head Master Chair, I turn the setting up two notches on the vibrator. Her moans soon fill the space. The view from the platform is doing no justice to the moans escaping her. I stand and pace the room for a minute. Interested, I need to get a closer view of her body, needing to see the juices dripping from her pussy as she cums. No other client gets me as close to the edge as her. The others usually say some dumb shit, moan unnecessarily loud, or do something that keeps me in professional mode. Bunny, on the other hand, her vibe is effortlessly sensual. Her submissiveness overwhelms me at times. She has the ability to humbly exhaust me both mentally and physically. Not to her knowledge, I hope. Don't think I could handle any woman knowing they have that much control over me.

I see that she's nearing the edge again. My anticipation builds from not only watching her, but also hearing her cum. It didn't take her long to catch a second orgasm. Her moans turn into grunts as she releases.

I stump my boot to frighten her. "Who told you to cum? I didn't give you permission. Did I? Next time, you ask me to orgasm."

I remove the vibrator from her clit, gripping her waist to enter her from behind. Her pussy is sopping wet. So wet, I slide in her swollen pussy with ease. I slowly stroke her, allowing her walls to adjust to my dick. Next, I dig in to her deeper until her back arches. I pull out slowly, leaving her there until she begs for me.

"Please, please. Please Boots!"

Intentionally, I ignore her pleas. It's time to turn this up a notch. I owe her a few punishments for disobeying my orders earlier. She won't get off that easy tonight. We are barely 45 minutes into the 2-hour session, and I'm losing control fast. On the fly, I try to think of something to prolong my erection. Scanning around the room, I notice the bottle of organic honey on the kitchen counter that I used earlier when making a cup of ginseng tea. It's a natural tea I picked up from an Asian grocery store. It works better than any libido pill I have tried. It supplies energy and boosts the libido without any side effects.

"Yeah, this should do the trick." I walk over, take the honey jar, and place it on the glass coffee table in the living room. I debate if the time is right to present Bunny's surprise, but I decide against it. The vibe isn't where it should be quite yet. I need to have a little more fun with her first.

I walk over to the bed and release Bunny from the cuffs, picking her up and throwing her over my shoulder. Her body hangs over my shoulder like a rag doll, so I plop her down on the living room couch. "Open your mouth. And leave it open."

She sits before me blindfolded, mouth open waiting on my next instruction. Deliberately, I step on her toes with my boots. Her face scrunches. Bunny grimaces from the pain. I know her feet hurt from wearing those heels all day. Like I said, I owe her a punishment or two.

The room grows quiet. That is, everything except her breathing. She's panting with her mouth ajar. I turn to pick up the honey from the table and dip two fingers in the jar. I scoop out a considerable amount. After smearing the thick and sticky honey on my dick, I place it directly in Bunny's face. I wait until her breathing calms. I know she feels my presence because her mouth opens wider in expectancy. I unhurriedly stick my dick in her mouth. "Suck my shit. Suck it until it's all gone."

There's no doubt she'll get the job done. Bunny takes me into her mouth with no hands. She works her lips around my dick, slurping loudly like it's hot ramen. Damn, I love the way she eats. Her tongue darts back and forth against the bottom of my shaft. That perfectly-applied shiny red lipstick she was wearing is now smeared around her mouth.

In the moment of ecstasy, I briefly close my eyes until her warm hands rub up my legs. I snap back into reality, knowing I still have a job to do. Her hands are searching to feel what her eyes can't see. The warm palm of her hand gently fondles my balls. Bunny massages them in her hand while never losing her rhythm, sucking my dick. She must have sucked the last remnants of sticky honey off my dick because her head lowers. She knows better than to disobey me at this point in the night.

Bunny flicks her wet warm tongue against my balls before taking them into her mouth. The light touch of her hand rubbing my gooch is driving me crazy. Her actions are aggressively pushing me further than I wanted to go. Should I stop her before I lose control of this session?

"Did I tell you to lick my balls, Bunny?" She stops mid-lick. Her tongue is hanging in the air. I push her head away. "Why do you disobey me? You really starting to piss me off."

What she doesn't know is that we will be checking off a few more of her sexual desires tonight. Before I do, I need to get her as close to the edge as possible, giving her no reason to say no or turn back.

"Lay down." I push her back against the couch. I fold her body with her knees nearly touching her lips. As I lower myself down onto the couch, I quickly ram my dick into her. With the blindfold still covering her eyes, I drill her hard. So hard, one of the anal beads pops out and drops to the floor. Fuck! The thought of her tight virgin ass sends a feeling through my body I've never felt before. All I know is I want her.

I ram her harder and harder. I say, "Spit it out!"

I listen intently for the second bead to hit the floor. Immediately, I pull out and demand her to stand up. I then take a seat where she just lain. My arms stretched along the back of the sofa, I say, "Turn around and sit on my dick." Still blindfolded, she turns, giving me an up-close view of her ass. Bunny gradually squats down onto my dick.

"No, I've already had your pussy." She freezes for a brief moment. The meaning of my words takes a few seconds to register in her mind. I want her to have control of this moment in hopes that the experience will be of pleasure more than resistance.

Bunny takes her time sitting her ass down on my dick, repeatedly, rising up and down, taking an inch at a time until the full eight inches disappear. Finally, she sits down on my lap. Her body is shaking nervously, but she proceeds anyway. Being the fast learner she is, she eases up and down my dick in one full stroke. Wasting no time, she starts bouncing on my dick like she did the first session. Her moans are loud as fuck. What the fuck? Why is she doing this to me? Feeling her ass contracting around my dick at a steady pace has me unsure I can last much longer. This is not how the night was supposed to go. I reach around her body to palm her breasts, squeezing them, burying my face in her spine.

Bunny asks, "Please may I cum? Please." She hops until she gets her fill. Her body trembles. Her moans send me over the edge. My orgasm nears, so I grab her waist thrusting my hips upward until I violently release.

I was so engrossed in watching her ass. I didn't look up at her face until now. The blindfold rests around her neck. With heavy breathing, she stares at the man sitting across the room. He stares back at her. Shit, I forgot about him just that quick. That's how easy I'm immersed when she's near.

When did she remove the blindfold? I can't read her face. No emotion. No signs of distress. She stands, slowly easing her ass off my dick before gathering her steps and stumbling into the bathroom.

Boots - Ch. 4

Again, this isn't how I planned this night would go. The plan was for him to observe how to properly dominate a woman. At the least, let him get his dick sucked. In his consultation, he introduced himself by the name Danny. Danny mentioned he's interested in domination and voyeurism. He wanted to take a step outside of porn and witness it in real life. He's the first male client of Just Boots.

Of course, I had my suspicions. My first thought was to ensure he wasn't the husband of any of my clients. Thoroughly, I searched through my clientele list, checked the backgrounds and the emergency contact information they provided. The results rendered no red flags. Because of my due diligence, the level of risk seemed improbable. On the outside, his looks scream "faithful executive type," but you can tell he has a fetish that he's unable fulfill on his own. The contract I proposed offered him permission to watch for $500 an hour. He accepted. In hopes of checking off another one of Bunny's sexual desires of a threesome, I would have let her suck his dick while I fucked her. But the night didn't go as planned. I got lost in the moment and temporarily forgot he was even there.

Although, the way she looked at him has me concerned. Was it shock or interest?

Without knocking, I walk into the bathroom and close the door. "Bunny, are you okay? Let me know if anything tonight made you uncomfortable." I pause. "You have permission to speak."

She gives a half-smile. "I'm okay. I was just shocked to see someone else here."

"Are you sure? I can remove any outside parties from your profile if you'd like. I don't want to upset you." My words are heartfelt and true. I wish I could see her outside of the loft, but I know we've overstepped those boundaries.

"Thank you. No, that won't be necessary. I'll be out in a few minutes." I nod to her, acknowledging her need for space. I exit the bathroom, gently closing the door behind me.

As I turn, Danny is walking towards me. He says, "Thank you for your time. It was more enjoyable than I could have expected. The way she orgasmed while looking at me. That is something I will never forget." The admiring way he speaks of Bunny is testing my manhood.

My brain is in overdrive. She orgasmed while looking at him? What the fuck, Bunny? I try to shake off my possible misperception. "Glad you enjoyed it my man. You have my card."

"Yes, I do. Thank you." We shake hands before he exits the huge steel door. I stare at the door, puzzled by his declaration, attempting to sort my thoughts. Why am I so angry right now? No, definitely not jealously. Couldn't be.

I slam the steel door and turn on my heels to confront Bunny, only to find her standing behind me. I ask, "Did he make you cum? Did you waste my fucking time tonight?"

"Huh, what are you talking about? No. No, I had a great time with you tonight."

Why is she evading my question? I repeat myself. "Did he make you cum, Bunny?"

"Boots, NO! I was just so close when the blindfold fell. I just. I just couldn't stop." Her answer might be legit, but why do I feel so disrespected? I shake my head at the thought of her, him, *them* both playing me.

I pace back and forth, before facing her. "You should go," I say. No other words escape me, although there's so much more I want to say.

Bunny asks, "Did I do something? You seem mad?" She gently touches my arm.

"Let's just end the night here. You can go now," I reply, opening the steel door.

She stares at me with a look of disbelief. After a few seconds of silence, she exits without turning back.

Boots - Ch. 5

For some reason, this Monday is more hectic than usual. The office is closed today, but business hasn't slowed. There were two new consultations last week in addition to my normal appointments. I finally have a day to catch up on reading emails, financials, and appointment scheduling. I release a sigh of frustration after noticing the email icon displaying 54 unread emails. Instead of wasting time opening them all, I quickly read over the subject and sender. One email grasps my attention. The subject line simply reads, 'Sorry'. I click open the email.

Boots,

How are you? I want to apologize for not giving you notice after not scheduling appointments for the past couple of months. Thank you for the boundless experiences. You are the greatest at what you do. My body will never forget you. Your dick, your words, your touch will forever be etched in my mind.

I also regrettably wanted to say that my husband hired someone to follow me a few months ago. He found out about Just Boots. My husband hired a private investigator to get a closer look into what I was doing at your loft. As you have probably guessed, this turned out to be the guy in the room last time we were together. I am so so sorry. I truly had no idea. Remember I was late that day? Well, my husband tried picking a fight before my meeting with you. Looking back, I assume he wanted to stop me from seeing you, but I wasn't going to cancel my time with you. Although, I really like you and would like to see you again. I know I can't. We're trying to work things out. Boots you are truly everything I could ask for sexually. You will always hold a special place in my heart.

XOXO my Orgasm King!
Bunny

I bury my face in my hands. This seems like a joke. Why did my favorite client have to get caught up? When she didn't schedule an appointment last month, I knew something wasn't right. Many different scenarios ran through my head. Maybe she was mad at me for acting the way I did. I knew I was wrong for accusing her of wasting my time. I thought maybe she could be pregnant or getting a divorce. If I would have known that would be the last time I'd see her, I wouldn't have ended the session the way I did.

It never occurred to me someone would go through such lengths to hire a private investigator. Honestly, I have to acknowledge her husband's genius. He's much smarter than I could have expected. What I do know is that he doesn't deserve her, probably never will. I know she still wants to see me. If only I can get her back in my sight, at least one last time. She needs me. She's my muse. Contemplating her words over again, I now realize this job is no longer fun without her.

I hit reply to her message.

Need to see you. Anytime. Anywhere.

Valentine's Day

It's the official day of love. The infamous Valentine's Day! A dreaded day for some. A celebration of love for others. Women usually plan the same old thing for their lucky guy. There's dinner. Lingerie. Guaranteed sex. But not me! I'm planning something special for my fiancé of six months. My man is the best lover in my world. He deserves some extra attention. He works hard, provides, pampers, and tends to my needs often. He's a man of action and proves himself every day. I try to be his 'more than enough', but sometimes feel he does more for me than I do for him. So, today is about showing him how I feel and giving him a day he deserves.

Valentine's Day - Ch. 2

6:42 a.m.

I roll over in bed, hoping not to wake him. Sleep didn't come easy knowing what the day has in store. There's much to do today. First up, a surprise breakfast! I rise from the bed and discretely creep into the bathroom, attempting to quietly release my bladder without waking Babe. I brush my teeth, wash my face, and remove my hair bonnet.

My plan should work as he is an extremely heavy sleeper. Hopefully he doesn't feel my presence missing. It's that feeling when the bed gets cold and unfamiliar, and it wakes you. Since we've met, we cuddle all night, making it difficult to sleep without one another. Quietly, I open the door and glance over to find him still sleeping.

I tip toe out of the room and head downstairs to prepare his favorite breakfast of strawberry cream stuffed French toast. I'll include a side of bacon and fresh squeezed grapefruit juice to top it off. I remove the bacon, eggs, milk, cream cheese, and butter from the fridge. Next, I fetch bread from the pantry.

After turning on the heat for the griddle and frying pan, I crack three eggs into a shallow dish, adding in a little milk, vanilla extract, cinnamon, and nutmeg. Then, I set it aside while I prepare the stuffing mixture. I slice and chop the fresh strawberries. I add bacon to the hot pan. I mix the cream cheese and chopped strawberries in a bowl, placing a hefty amount between two bread slices. Next, I dip the French toast in the batter and place the slices on the griddle. Once he smells the bacon, it won't be long before he makes his way to the kitchen.

As expected, as I turn over the bacon and French toast, he treads downstairs rubbing the sleep from his eyes. "Happy Lover's Day to you," I say.

"Thank you, baby. Happy Lover's Day to you, too. I thought you said you only wanted to do dinner this year?" He says with a raspy voice.

I pour a small amount of syrup in a small pot to warm. "I know. But you've been such a good boy, thought you needed some appreciation today… and today just so happens to fall on Valentine's Day." I pause briefly to snicker. "I have a few things planned… starting off with your favorite breakfast. Have a seat."

When I plan something, he knows to expect the unexpected. He gives me a sneer before he sits at the breakfast bar. I remove the French toast from the griddle and put it directly onto a plate. I then place a few strips of the drained bacon on his plate. He looks at me with a sly grin when I serve his plate and pour the warmed syrup over his French toast.

"Blackberry? Give me." I turn from the stove to find him motioning for a kiss by pursing his lips and leaning over the counter. I lean in, giving him a quick peck on the lips. When we cook for one another, we make sure to kiss the cook. Of course, that's usually me, but I pay my dues when he attempts.

"Thank you, baby!" He blesses his food and digs in. I fix a small plate for myself and sit beside him. He glances over at me. "Wish you would've told me you wanted to do something today. I could've planned something special for you baby." He takes a bite of bacon. "We still on for dinner though, right?"

"You always doing nice things for me though. You tend to me all the time."

"I know, but I feel bad I didn't do anything. I bet you have the whole day planned, huh?" he responds.

"I'm not saying. Just enjoy your breakfast, nosy!"

Valentine's Day - Ch. 3

7:58 a.m.

After breakfast, I hurry cleaning in hopes of catching him in the shower. There's one more plan in store before he heads to the office this morning. He's co-owner of an architecture firm located in downtown Dallas. After college, he partnered with a friend he interned with. They have been in business for four years. I'm proud of his drive and well-earned accomplishments.

When I open the bathroom door, the shower is still running. I quietly remove my clothes before opening the shower door. He wipes his face and looks at me with a surprised smile. He's squinting through his left eye because of the water in his right.

"Need some help?" I ask seductively.

With a lustful gaze he says, "What you doing? Swear you trying to make me late. Baby, I don't have time."

"Babe, you own the joint. You can be a little late. If you don't interrupt me again this shouldn't take long." My assertive words take him by surprise. Standing on my toes, I lean in to kiss his perfectly soft lips. Trailing light kisses down his neck, then to his stomach, then kneeling with the water running down my back. I lick my lips and slowly take him in mouth. Normally, there's more foreplay, but not today.

He curses aloud, "Shit." Hearing him moan is more than enough motivation to do my best. I focus on the head of his dick before slowly taking him into my mouth. I love his dick from the size, to the color, and especially the taste. Everything about it.

For his entertainment, I swallow as much as my little mouth can handle. Babe enjoys hearing me gag and choke on his big dick. He grunts loudly and says, "Keep going."

My hands grip and stroke him into my mouth. The pace increasing when I feel him growing harder. I give him a doe-eyed look to see the enjoyment on his face. He grabs the back of my head and forces his dick further down my throat. He fucks my mouth hard before growling and convulsing, and leaving me to swallow a mouthful of warm cum. He reaches out for the shower wall for support. I stand and wipe my mouth with the back of my hand, stepping out of the shower without saying a word.

Valentine's Day – Ch. 4

11:45 a.m.

I finish my morning errands of shopping for a new, little black dress for our dinner date tonight. My schedule is cleared of all appointments today to dedicate time for what I hope is one of his best days ever. I want to give him memories he will never forget.

He doesn't usually schedule meetings during lunch hours, so it proves a perfect time to plan an impromptu date. At noon, his assistant is expected to hand him an envelope I prepared. The card in the envelope has only an address and two instructions.

Don't use google. Enter the address in the car GPS only.

My phone chirps and the car's Bluetooth informs me there's an incoming text from Babe. I stop at the traffic light to read his message.

Babe: *What you up 2 woman?*
Me: *Just meet me there. And don't cheat (side-eyed emoji)*
Babe: *(tongue out emoji) ok boss. Leaving now*

Fifteen minutes later, I hurry to exit the building towards the entrance to wait for him. A few minutes after that, his black

Corvette speeds into the parking lot. He parks and steps out of the car. Seeing his fine ass strut towards me instantly makes me horny. I wave to gain his attention. A huge smile covers his face when he sees me. There's no way he would've expected this surprise.

"Hey baby," he says placing a sweet kiss on my lips.

"So… what do you think?" I extend my arms towards the building for dramatic affect.

"Can't believe you remembered. I've been wanting to visit since they opened last year. I'm for real kinda giddy right now." He rubs his hands together in anticipation.

With a smile, I say, "I knew you would be! Let's go in." We enter the African Artifacts Museum. He's studied African artifacts and culture since college. Our home is filled with books and collectibles.

We stroll the museum enjoying each other's company. I enjoy hearing him speak so passionately. He stops to examine each display, giving me a synopsis of its origin and cultural significance. I begin to realize how mentally stimulated he has become by his physical touch subconsciously reflecting his feelings. There's the subtle grabbing of my hand and resting his hand on my hip. Not to mention the wicked look in his eyes.

Near the end of the tour, I suggest, "Let's stop by the gift shop." Beforehand, I provided the manager a wrapped gift to surprise him. Hope it goes as planned. We look over the mass-produced t-shirts and replica knickknacks. I call over the cashier and ask if this is all they have for sale. She says, "Yes, but I can ask the manager if we have more." We stride towards the checkout counter. The manager and cashier return with the wrapped gift.

He looks around the room curiously. The manger greets us. "Hi, how are you two today? We have a special artifact not many people have seen. I believe someone special wanted you to have this," she says handing him the gift.

"What's this?" He looks at me with a curious look.

Giving him my best perplexed look, "Open it." He unwraps a rare Ghanaian painting of slaves in a dungeon awaiting trade from the 1500s. Retrieving the painting was expensive and required secured transport, but it was all worth it. His face is of pure shock, exhilaration, and slight sadness. He reaches over and gives me a long hug, repeatedly whispering thank you in my ear.

"Thank you, baby! This is extraordinary! I don't really know what to say. Thank you so much." My heart melts seeing the appreciation in his eyes. My mission is to fill him with that type of happiness for the rest of our lives.

After the heart-tugging moment in the gift shop, we make our way back to the parking lot. While walking me to my car he says, "Don't forget we have dinner plans at eight. You have to be on time tonight, okay?"

"Okay, okay! Do you want me to pull something for you to wear?"

"Naw, let me take it from here, Berry. This day has been damn near perfect. Let me handle the rest. Cool?" He repeats himself because I won't lay off unless he enforces me to.

With a sly smile, "If you insist. Can we at least try the new toy I bought though?"

"Yo, you be wilding! But yea, we can try it."

I say, "You don't even know what it is. You just down for whatever, huh?"

"I trust you." He gives me a hug and places a sensual kiss on my lips before he returns to his car.

Valentine's Day - Ch. 5

7:13 p.m.

"**Y**ou almost ready? We need to leave here in like twenty minutes."

I finish applying the dark red lipstick. "I know. You've reminded me five times already. Just need to put on my dress. Can you help me please?" He looks at me through the mirror.

"You look beautiful. Now, can you hurry up so we don't lose our reservation." He is such a perfectionist. Also, a stickler for time. I both like and dislike that about him. He's always rushing me. At the same time, I know he'll always be there when he says he will.

I pull the new little black dress off the hanger and step into the dress. "Zip me up, please? Where are we going anyway? You still haven't told me."

He winks then slowly moves the zipper up over my ass. Without saying a word, he leaves the bedroom. "Really?" I say aloud. Guess that means I need to hurry. I settle on a pair of six-inch black strappy stilettos and a small black clutch to compliment the dress. Hurriedly, I fill the purse and grab my phone before heading downstairs.

"Okay, I'm ready!"

He stands near the TV with the remote in one hand and a glass of bourbon in the other. I have his undivided attention as I descend the stairs. At the wet bar, he sits down his glass, picks up something, and sneaks it behind his back.

"Damn baby," he whistles. "You look good." He meets me at the bottom of the staircase and hugs me tight. "There something I want you to wear though." He hands me a black box.

"A gift? What is it? Jewelry?" I ask.

He gives me stern look. "Need you to follow my instructions. You listening?"

A heavy sigh lingers in the air. He knows me too well. "Ugh yeah, I'm listening."

"Go to the bathroom and put this on. You have five minutes to return back to me."

"Five minutes?"

He gives me a 'don't play with me' look. "Yes sir. I'll be back." I hand him my purse and turn to make my way to the half bath down the hall. I take my time opening the gift but remember he only gave me five minutes. Ripping open the box, I give it an inquisitive look. Why is a piece missing? I see a small black piece of cloth. I open the instruction book and gasp. "Oh my," I say aloud, finally realizing it's a remote-controlled vibrating thong toy thingy, and he has control of the remote. "This about to be a eventful night!"

∞ ∞ ∞

We park at the valet of a small slightly hidden restaurant. "I've never been here before. How'd you find this place?" I ask.

"I met the Williams brothers here for lunch when the firm won the media company contract. I knew I had to bring you here one day. Think you'll really like it," he says as we walk towards the entrance.

He opens the door. Immediately, I'm in love. Upon entry, the sights and smells engulf you. It's beautiful and romantic. My head is on a swivel absorbing the beauty of the décor and architecture. Babe provides his name to the hostess to locate our reservation. Next, we are guided to our table near an imported Italian water fountain. The dim lights and candles offer a calming vibe. Beautiful green leafy vines cover the walls providing great contrast to the white chairs and linens.

"I must say this is very nice, baby. Feels like we've been transported to someplace in Italy. It's so beautiful!"

The smile on his face says it all. Internally, he's probably patting himself on the back. "Glad you like it, beautiful." He pauses. "It's about time we finally plan that trip. Don't you think?"

Happily, I reply, "We've been talking about it for a long while. I'm more than ready!"

He smiles, "Glad you said that because I planned us a two-week vacation there for your birthday next month." He removes a black envelope from his pocket and hands it to me. It's two first-class tickets to Italy. He asks, "You like it?"

My eyes water from the overwhelming joy. I lean across the table to kiss his face. "Yes! I'm so happy right now. Thank you so much baby. I can't wait." My hand covers my heart.

I calm myself and wipe my eyes. I pick up my menu. "Hope the food is as good as it smells. You've been here before. What'd you suggest?"

"I mean, everything sounds appetizing. I tried the lobster ravioli appetizer and the chicken parm last time, and it was amazing."

The waitress approaches our table. We order a bottle of vintage red wine, the lobster ravioli appetizer, and house salads to start. For entrees, he orders the chicken parmesan for himself and the lobster risotto for me.

We engage in light conversation over dinner. As expected, the food is amazing. The night is dynamic. I ponder why he hasn't used the remote yet. I've been on edge the entire dinner waiting for him to at least acknowledge what he's started. I even tried bringing up the topic in the car on the way here, but he changed the subject. Now, the anticipation is killing me. What was the purpose if he didn't plan to use it?

Just as the annoyance uprises, a slow vibration stimulates my clitoris. Abruptly, I sit down my glass of wine, trying not spill it. My breathing is hurried and my mouth slightly parts. The waitress approaches our table. "Would you like to order dessert tonight?" I see his mouth moving, but I can't comprehend what he's saying.

"Baby? Babe?"

I snap out of the trance he placed me in. The pleasure down below is intercepting signals allowing me to think properly. "Huh? I'm so sorry. What did you say?" I ask.

He gives a sly naughty smile. "You, okay? She asked if you wanted to try any desserts?"

I shift in my chair and look at the young waitress. She appears perplexed. Her head turning from me to him, back to me again. I smile at her and ask she give us a few minutes to look over the dessert menu. She nods and gives me a wink as she turns away. Did she sense the sexual tension in the air?

I lean in to whisper across the table, "You're so wrong for that. Why'd you wait until now? I think she knew something was up." Just as I grab the dessert menu, he increases the intensity. A quiet moan escapes my lips. I don't suspect anyone heard over the Italian music playing throughout the restaurant. Through tattered breaths, I ask him if we should order anything to go.

"Whatever you want. I already know what I want for dessert," he says seductively.

"And what's that?"

"Ice cream," he replies.

He just shrugs his shoulders. I can't sense if he's joking or not. We both laugh at the silliness—and tension—of the conversation.

Valentine's Day – Ch. 6

9:42 p.m.

We exit the restaurant, bellies full of good food and good wine. The temperature has dropped a few degrees since we first entered the restaurant. I snuggle up to him. "Thank you, baby, for dinner. I really enjoyed today. How about you?"

"Definitely one the best days I've ever had." He grabs my hand. "Let's walk before we pick up the car."

I look down at the three-inch black heels on my feet. "Uh… Okay."

We stroll down the block. It seems like the perfect time to use the remote again, in my opinion. I guess not so much for him. Before I can offer my suggestion, he stops in front of a local ice cream shop.

"Come on, they're still open." An older gentleman greets us as we enter the shop and informs us to let him know when we're ready to order.

We approach the counter to see what flavors are available. "You were serious about wanting ice cream?" I ask. After we laughed about it, I assumed he was just making a joke or playing around. His actions are surprisingly unpredictable tonight. Just when I think I know him, he does things like this to keep me on my toes.

"You didn't believe me? Told you what I wanted." He places his hand in his pocket and sets the vibration on the highest intensity. I drop my head and try to steady myself. There's no music here to drown out my moans, so I bite my lip to restrain my cries.

He tightens his hand around my waist to help hold me up. I give him a pleading look to take me home.

"Sir, we'll just have a cone of the chocolate soft serve. Glad we caught you before you closed." He converses with the older man while he prepares the order. His demeanor is cool and calm. All the while, my body tingles all over. My panties are soaked and cold. The prolonging of this night will only drive me nuts. The older man gives him the cone in exchange for a ten-dollar bill. He tells the man to keep the change. As we exit the shop, the vibration stops.

I release an exhausting sigh. "Whew, what are trying to do to me? You better hope this thing don't electrocute me." I playfully hit his arm. "So… I don't get any ice cream?"

"My bad. You want some?" He extends the cone out to me. I reach out to grab it, and he snatches his hand back. "Nope, no hands," he directs.

What is up with him tonight? With attitude, I place a hand on my hip. "What? Are you serious? Right here?" I look up and down the lively sidewalk.

"Yep, you want some or not?"

I nod my head yes. He extends the cone to me again. I open wide and take the tip of the ice cream into my mouth, slowly slurping it up.

"Hmph… You nasty!" He chuckles. "Didn't think you was gonna do it. That was kinda sexy though," he says with a wide smile. "Come on woman, let's head home."

Valentine's Day - Ch. 7

10:24 p.m.

The car ride home was surprisingly quiet, except the mix of 90's slow jams playing. His hand on my thigh or a quick glance over at me, but nothing more than that. Maybe the words we didn't speak weren't needed. Maybe our thoughts occupied the same space, substituting words with no meaning.

He pulls into the garage and turns off the car. We enter the house silently. I pass him on my way into the kitchen, as he disarms the alarm. Placing my purse on the oversized island and removing my heels, he approaches me from behind. His hug is tight and possessive. He immediately lifts up my dress and layers kisses on my neck.

"Umm," I muster to say. All of the sentiments, the anticipation, the sexual tension of the entire day has led up to this moment.

I turn to face him. The hunger in his eyes is obvious. He leans in to kiss me. The slow and sensual kissing, quickly changing to fast and passionate within seconds. Our hands roam and tug at whatever piece of clothing will come off. He abruptly pulls away, leaving me in bewilderment. My lips instantly missing his. With his eyes on me, he eases down to his knees in front of me.

"Baby, what you doing?" I ask in a soft tone. Our heavy breathing echoes the silent room. His hands gingerly rub up my legs to my ass cheeks. He removes my thong panties and exposes my pussy to his face. I lift my left leg over his shoulder. Without hesitation, he dives in, covering my pussy with his mouth. My head falls back in ecstasy.

The moans can no longer be contained. "Oh baby! Mmm!" I plead for more, begging to cum. He applies pressure with the flat of his tongue. My pussy throbs from the steady strokes up and down against my clit.

"Please don't stop." My body tenses and tingles from my head to my toes as the orgasm approaches. I inhale a large breath of air. "I'm about to cum."

The uncontrollable contracting of my walls causes me to quiver and tremble against him. He continues sucking on my clit. "Oh my god! Baby, please. I can't." I beg him to stop nibbling on the sensitive bud. He stands and aggressively turns me around. He bends me over the counter and swiftly unzips his pants. He pulls them down and enters me slow, teasing me with the tip of his dick. I crave the feel of his bare skin entering my swollen wet pussy.

"FUCK," he yells. He repeatedly pulls out and re-enters me, each time he pumps harder and harder. He feels so good inside me. His hard, thick dick against my tight walls. My toes barely touch the floor. My left foot searches to find the footrest on the nearby barstool. I lift myself up and crawl further onto the counter. Babe climbs on top of the counter too, chasing what's his. He fucks me hard. So hard the decorative vase of flowers crashes to the floor. I think the sound of shattered glass only increased the desire burning between us.

"Ah, you feel so good," he declares.

I arch my back for more. He slips in and out with ease, creating sloppy wet sounds with each stroke. He groans and grips my shoulder, fucking me wildly.

"Yea, take it. It's yours," I say.

I grind my hips to match his aggression. He grunts loudly. With one last thrust, he fills me with his seed. His release is long and hard. His chest collapses against my back.

We both lay on the counter panting, finally relieved from the buildup throughout the day. He pulls out and jumps down off the counter. His pants barely hang from his left ankle. In between shallow breaths, he says, "Sorry, you didn't get to try your toy."

I glance at the time on the stove. "What do you mean? Valentine's Day not over yet!"

The Talk

Is it possible that a phone call could ruin everything? Reclining in my office chair, I scroll through the contacts in my phone to find his name. I've done this a few times already today, dreading the call, wishing I could delay it for another day. The phone rings loudly through the speaker and the moment I hear his voice, I consider whether what I have to say is worth saying. Is it worth losing him over this?

"Hey, beautiful."

I reply while also trying to steady my voice, "Hey, baby. How's your day going?"

Marin chuckles. "Hot. This heat is not funny. I have one more job after this one. How you doing?"

"I'm okay." I pause, working up the courage to continue the conversation. "Hey, I think we need to talk."

The silence on the other end frightens me.

"V, everything okay? Talk about what?" Marin asks. The concern in his voice makes me want to swallow my words but they're out there now, hanging between us like a web.

"I just think we need to discuss some things."

"Vanessa, usually when a woman says she wants to talk, it's not a good thing."

He's right, it's true, but I don't want him to assume the worst. "Umm, it's not necessarily bad. What time are you coming by tonight?" I ask.

He exhales a deep breath. The vague response I provided didn't seem to ease his worries. "I'll be there after I leave the gym. Probably around seven or eight."

"Okay, babe. We can talk then?" Hearing the frustration in his voice, I ask it more as a question to ease the suspense. He could easily cancel instead of dealing with me, but I'm wishing he won't.

His response is short and dry. "Yeah, see you then."

Marin is a really great man. We've dated for the past three months and it's tough to imagine not knowing him. Nor do I care to remember my life before him. It's not a picture-perfect love story, but it's our story and that's what makes it perfect in its own way. We met on a Friday night at a Mexican restaurant in Inglewood. I stood at the counter looking over the menu waiting to place a to-go order. A bell chimed, and when the entrance door opened, an extremely handsome man with light brown skin and a goatee walked in. He was covered in dirt, with work gloves hanging from his back pocket suggesting he must've just gotten off from work.

He picked up a menu and waited to place an order. Daring, I asked, "Have you been here before?" He told me it was his first time. He mentioned he'd just finished a landscaping job nearby and was looking to pick up dinner. We made light conversation while looking over the menu. I don't know if he was being audacious or just a friendly guy, but he asked if I wanted to join him for dinner. Luckily, I said yes. We ate and talked for hours. After a few margaritas, we laughed and cracked jokes like we had known each other forever. After dinner, he asked for my number and we've talked nearly every day since. After about a month, we decided to date exclusively. The relationship moved fast, but felt right.

The timing of our meeting was unreal. He was on the dating scene, ready to meet someone. It just so happened to be nearly a year since the ending of my previous, three-year relationship. It's still amazing how we were both ready for something serious.

The greatest part of our relationship is the fun we have together. We truly enjoy each other's company. His demeanor is serious, but he has a goofy side and doesn't mind playing around. I mean that in a childlike, curious kind of way. We play board games and cards. We make up our own silly games and handshakes. We even place sports bets against each other. On date nights, we visit different restaurants in the city with non-American cuisines, just to try something new. With him, fate definitely feels real. I know I've found my person.

But...there's one area where we don't align. To put it lightly, the sex is not what I expected. He's so caring and attentive, I assumed it would carry over into the bedroom but it hasn't. If I don't say something now, I know I'll regret it later.

After we had been dating exclusively for about a month and agreeing to only spend time with one another, I mentioned I wasn't ready to go there sexually. I didn't want to confuse the sexual intimacy for emotional intimacy. He said he was okay with waiting, replying jokingly with, "not too long, though." In my mind, I was thinking the exact same thing but I needed the boundary. The same way he needed his alone time.

Last weekend, we planned an overnight trip to Catalina Island. We spent the entire day touring, dined on the water, then had drinks at a bar near our hotel. Overall, it was a beautiful day. By the end of the night, I hoped the memorable day would take our relationship to the next level. I was ready for some physical attention and hoped he was too. We showered separately before lying down to watch a movie. He began rubbing on me, which led to us kissing and eventually our clothes came off. I admired his perfectly gorgeous dick. I eyed it to be about seven inches long, with descent girth. I just wanted to touch it, feel it in my hand. But that's not what happened.

The room had a nervous energy like we were sixteen losing our virginity. Marin removed a condom from his wallet and covered his shaft. He settled on top of me and began to penetrate me. No, I did not miss a step. There was no foreplay. I was barely wet enough for him to slide in. In hopes of getting my juices flowing, I pulled him down to kiss me but he was on a mission. He went to work and orgasmed in about twenty or thirty strokes. I laid there in shock for about two minutes. This couldn't be the same man I'd been getting to know. I asked him about orgasming quickly. His response was he was overly excited and didn't expect to cum so fast. It happens sometimes. Right?

The following Monday, we try again. After working late grading papers and preparing lessons, I drive from Sherman Oaks to his townhouse in Culver City. I convinced myself into believing it was nerves or the anticipation of our first time. Unfortunately, that was not the case. He guided me to his bedroom, removed my clothes, and laid me on the bed. He kisses me slowly before trailing kisses down to my soft spot. I thought to myself, "Yes! He's taking his time!"

Yet, what happens next is torture. He pulls back the hood to expose my sensitive clit, harshly flicking the tip of his tongue. I grip the sheets to keep from screaming, and not in a good way. It was painful, my body slowly backed up to relieve the tension.

So instead, I say, "I want you inside of me." Gratefully, he pauses to retrieve a condom and climbs back on top of me. Again, he entered my pussy in one full stroke. He pumped on me for about five to seven minutes before he finished.

I'm still trying to figure out how he didn't pick up on my body language. I should have said something or guided him, but I really like him and didn't want to hurt his feelings. But the truth is, I just didn't know him well enough to comprehend how much his ego could handle.

Now, it's been four days since we last had sex. I want us to work badly, which is why I called him today. With any luck, the conversation will go well, allowing us to fix our issues. On the other hand, he could reject me and never want to talk to me again. He could claim I'm the one with the issue. I like him enough to grow through this together. I hope he sees that.

A text message appears on my phone. Marin lets me know he's on the way. Luckily, I made it home from work with just enough time to cook a light dinner and shower. I pour a glass of wine to calm my nerves. Many different scenarios are running through my mind. What if he tells me to fuck off? What if he realizes I am not what he wants? I ramble a silent prayer and hope for the best.

Marin knocks on the front door before letting himself in. "Baby?" He drops his bag by the door.

I exit the kitchen to greet him with a kiss. "Hey, handsome. How you doing?"

"Good. A little tired. It's been a long day. Everything okay with you?" He wraps his arms around my waist.

I break the embrace and return to the kitchen. I shout, "I'm okay. Come eat while it's still hot." I prepare him a dinner plate and pour him glass a of wine. I pour myself another.

We take a seat at the dining table. Marin's concern is written on his face. He knows I'm stalling. He refuses to let this drag on any longer. He sets his fork down before taking a bite. "V, come on with it. Just tell me what's up."

"Well, I don't really know how to say this."

He shakes his head. "Don't tell me you're about to say we're over?"

I look him in the eyes before replying. "No. No. That's not it. I really like you, Marin. I like you a lot. It's just…" The eye contact is so intense. Why is this so hard? I should've been better prepared for this. No amount of rehearsal could have prepped me for this type of vulnerability. "I just wanted to talk about our sexual relationship. It hasn't started out that well. Don't you think?"

He stuffs a couple of bites of food in his mouth. With an annoyed expression on his face, he looks up from his plate. "That's what you wanted to say? For real?"

"Yeah. I thought we could talk about it. I don't like being left unsatisfied. I don't want that for you either." I pause. "You weren't that good babe." Ugh, did I just say that?

He doesn't respond right away. He chews his food slowly. His face is void of expression. Oh no, he's mad at my comment. He swallows and takes a sip of wine, and with a slight cheekiness he replies, "Baby, you weren't that good either."

We stare at each other briefly before erupting in laughter.

With relief, I say. "That's so funny. I didn't even think of it from your perspective. I could see why you would say that actually. I was like a pillow princess, huh?" I recollect my actions during those nights. "So, what is it I did or didn't do?"

He chews the food in his mouth before responding. "It's not that I was expecting you to do something specific. I just wanted you to be more into me I guess."

"I'm definitely into you. You do know that right? You just moved so fast. I should've just asked you to slow down."

He nods his head. "Sorry about that. Shit, I was excited. New pussy will do that to you." He chuckles with food in his cheek.

Marin stands up from the table. He picks up his plate and wine glass and heads toward the kitchen. My eyes are glued on his tight ass and broad shoulders. I turn my head attempting to snap my attention from my wandering thoughts. He places his dishes in the sink. Next, he opens the fridge to retrieve a bottle of water. He drinks nearly the entire bottle before asking, "Okay. Tell me. What is it you like, baby? What can I do to make you happy?"

I ponder his question before replying. "Umm, let me ask you something first. Do you like getting your dick sucked? Just asking, cause some guys don't."

His eyes are glued on me as he returns to his seat. I think the directness of my question threw him for a loop. He leans back in his chair before answering, "Yeah. I do."

I flirt back with him. "Good."

A wide smile covers his face. "By the way, I enjoy foreplay. Can I please get a little more foreplay?"

After a few silent moments pass, he scoots his chair back from the table. "Come here, baby."

Unhurriedly, I stand from my chair and sashay over to him. Marin pulls me down to straddle his lap. He opens the short silk robe covering my body, revealing my matching black bra and panties. His eyebrows raise at the sight of my full breasts in front of his face. He leans in and kisses me softly. My hands massage his bald head, his neck, down to his shoulders. His hands freely roam over my body. Just as I begin to grind my hips against him, he breaks the kiss and grips my ass with both hands.

"Umm! I like that," I say in between kisses on his neck.

"Oh yeah, you like when I grab your ass like this?" He grips and massages my ass again.

"Umm hmm! I like it when you talk like that." I pull his shirt over his head. I'm liking the side of him very much.

He removes the robe from my shoulders. "Take this off. Let me see you."

Obediently, I remove the robe, then my bra. I drop them to the floor. He grabs my breasts taking a nipple into his mouth, but I pull away. We both examine the wet hardened flesh. He takes my nipple into his mouth again and gently bites down. "Ooh!" The overwhelming pleasure takes over my body. The moans grow louder. "Yes, suck harder!"

Without rising from his seat, he lifts me up from his lap, sitting me on the wooden dining table. Damn, he hasn't been playing around in the gym! My heart races with excitement. His behavior now proving he's the man I imagined he would be in bed.

Marin instructs me, "Lean back with your fine ass." I obediently follow his direction, leaning back with my forearms against the table. He pulls me to the edge of the table, placing my feet on his shoulders.

Through my panties, he caresses my clit with his thumb. "That feels good, Marin," I let him know I'm pleased.

"I like it when you say my name, V." He scoots up his chair eager to partake in the prepared feast. He trails kisses from my calf moving upward. Marin taps my thigh, silently demanding I raise my hips, so he can easily remove my panties.

"Kiss my pussy, Marin," I say staring into his eyes. He proceeds to do as asked, placing soft kisses on my pussy lips. His kisses are wet and sweet as he works his tongue. The French kisses send tingles up my spine. Just as my mind locks in, he pulls back the hood to expose my clit. I stop him before he begins flicking his tongue. "Marin," I beg, "Not yet. Save that for when I'm about to cum." I briefly pause. "Please baby?"

He nods his head. "Tell me how you like it." He says in between kisses to my clit.

"Place your fingers inside me."

He wets his index and ring finger and inserts them inside me. He fingers me until I stop him. "No, don't move your hand, only your fingers. Rub the top of my wall like this." I wag my fingers back and forth as if I asked him to come over. "I want you to feel what turns me on. Every time I grip your fingers, I want you to keep licking, and sucking, and doing what you're doing. Okay?"

Marin listens intently like a perfect student.

"Now, kiss my pussy again baby." I lie down with my back against the table.

His lips are cold, but his mouth is warm. My walls squeeze his fingers as soon as his warm tongue covers my clit. He moans, "You like that, huh?" He lightly darts his tongue up and down my clit. He's definitely a fast learner. He kisses my pussy again, then flicks his tongue against my clit. He does it over and over until my pussy tightly grips his fingers. My body shakes. My orgasm forcing his fingers out of me. I feel the juices drip down to my ass. With heavy breathing, I look up at him. His face is serious. He looks dazed. "Are you okay?" I ask with concern.

"Damn, I'm so fucking turned on right now." His hand rests on his dick. "No lie, I almost came too."

I offer my hand for assistance to sit up. I ease down from the table to stand in front of him. "Oh really. You would have to promise me a round-two if that happened."

He smiles, "I ain't going nowhere. It's whatever you want sweetheart."

Giving him my most seductive gaze, I kneel in front of him. I take the hand he used to finger me and place them in my mouth. I suckle on my own juices and watch him bite his bottom lip. He removes his wet finger from my mouth and reaches down to tease my nipple.

"Right now, it's whatever you want." I massage his calves, pausing to remove his shoes. I slide my hands underneath his shorts to rub his thighs. "Stand up," I direct him.

I gingerly pull down his gym shorts and briefs over his erection. My god, he's beautiful. It's criminal how bad I want him.

"Sit down." He steps out of his clothes and takes a seat. I lean in to kiss his stomach. "I want you to tell me how to make you cum."

"Huh?" he says curiously.

I speak into the mic, in between kisses, I repeat, "Tell me. How you. Like your. Dick sucked." Placing my hand at the base of his dick, I take the head into my mouth. Sucking like a blow pop.

He says, "Take it all into your mouth." I go forth with gusto tasting all of him.

"Slowly baby!" As instructed, I slow my pace.

He says, "Aah! Yea, just like that!"

"Do it again." I stop and lick the head.

"Again."

"Swallow that shit."

It's a turn on hearing how much he's enjoying my attempt to please him.

Marin runs his hand through my hair. "Use your hands baby. Stroke me into your mouth." I moan with a mouthful. My hands twisting up and down, grinding his shaft. He raises his hips against my hand. "Damn, baby. Yeah. Suck that shit."

I stroke at a steady pace until his body becomes rigid. "Shit, baby," he says.

He puts his hand on my chin in attempts to pull my mouth away. His cum fills my mouth, and I appreciatively swallow his gift. The thick sticky fluid coats the back of my throat.

Grinning, I say, "That was fun."

With labored breath he questions, "Where'd it go?"

"I swallowed it."

He smiles, "No you didn't."

"I did. Where else you think I put it? You said swallow it." I hold up my hands in surrender and stick out my tongue.

Marin shakes his head with a huge grin on his face. He stands and holds out his hand to help me off my knees. His voice is low and mischievous. "Come on. We gotta finish this conversation in the bedroom." Marin slaps my ass. "I got more I need to say."

Pay to Play

"**I** think I'm going to call." The words blurt from my mouth. My best friend, Jennisha, sits down beside me on the outdoor sofa. She places the newly opened bottle of red wine on the glass top coffee table. The cool breeze blows her long, wavy extensions across her face. "Did you hear me?" I ask.

She gives an exasperated sigh. "Uh, yeah I heard you. You already know what you want to do, so do it. You still my friend even if you hire a male escort to knock you off," she giggles, amused by her own comedy.

Maybe she's right. True enough, I researched an agency for weeks before spilling the tea to her. This website named One for All advertises how they provide escort services for high-paying clientele and how their selection can meet any need or fantasy. It could be exactly what I need after my divorce last year. I hoped Jennisha would provide some honest insight or advice before I move forward with this crazy idea I formed in my mind.

My ex-husband, Savion, and I divorced a year ago after six years of marriage. Luckily, we were well-off financially, so the split of assets didn't cause a rift during the divorce proceedings. However, the separation from Savion wrecked my romantic life. He is a lying cheater, and I refused to touch him after finding out about his lil side chick. Now, it's been nearly two years since placing my hands on a dick. The time has come to take back control of my life, but the dating scene is now foreign territory.

Jen shifts in her seat, positioning her body to face me. "Listen Cincy, I'm here for whatever you want to do. You know that. I just hoped you'd try to meet someone in the normal way. Like at the coffee shop, a bar, or something. But hey, I understand why you want to try something new. I might need a little something on the side too. BJ barely want to fuck anymore. His young old ass don't have no extra energy."

I fold over in laughter. Listening to her complain about her husband is hilarious. They were high school sweethearts. I think back to when we met in college and how simple life was back then. Now, we're nearing our 30s and life has completely changed for us all.

"Well, Jen you know how hard that man works. Cut him a break. You might just need to pull out the tricks again. You know what he likes. I'm just saying. That might get his attention."

"Yeah. You might be right. But I need to think of something new though. Like maybe role-play or something! We haven't tried that yet. Shit, we haven't tried anything in a while. If you have any ideas, please gimme."

Shrugging my shoulders, "I don't know. Girl, find something you think he'll like. I tried role-playing once with an ex before you know who." I pause to take a sip of wine. "This one time we acted like strangers at a nightclub. We ended up making out, then fucked by his car in the parking lot."

The look of shock on Jen's face is priceless. Her jaw is on the floor. "You did what! Oh, my goodness. Damn I need to try that! Girrrlll!"

"Thought I told you that before. I miss that kind of spontaneity. Savion would never do anything like that. He feels like such a waste of time. Promise you, I'm about to get back out there though." Jen looks at me with pursed lips. "I'm for real Jen. Gonna hire me a fine little something to do what Savion didn't do."

She holds her hand in the air for us to high-five in celebration. "Okay, I hear you. You do that because I want to hear all about it!"

"You already know!"

Jen drinks a large gulp of wine. "Let me get out of here before BJ start blowing me up for being out too late, even though it's only 9:45 p.m. You know how he get."

We stand from the sofa and embrace in a hug. "Okay friend. Thanks for coming over," I say while clearing the wine glasses from the table.

Jennisha opens the patio door to enter the house. "Anytime. Cici, let me know how it goes."

We walk towards the front door to say our goodbyes. "You know I will. Get home safe."

Pay to Play – Ch. 2

Two weeks later . . .

Thursday approached quickly. The work week has been hectic, causing the days to fly by faster than usual. I've finally found some downtime. The bright light from my laptop shines upon my face. I read the company's mission statement aloud, "One for All specializes in finding the something or someone for anyone." In hopes it serves true, I click the sign-up button. "Hmph. We'll see about that."

I nervously take a sip of vino, seeking a little liquid courage to calm my erratic nerves. "Here goes nothing!" The registration is quite simple. After providing my personal data, it asks, "Why are you interested in joining One for All?" Pondering the question, the answer doesn't seem as simple as assumed. My original reason was to get fucked, have some fun, and get fucked again. Now, I'm not so sure, because in the moment I feel insecure and slightly embarrassed. People do this all the time, right? What if I don't have sex, but instead meet someone special and that leads to sex? Maybe Jen was right; I should just meet someone the old-fashioned way.

Why are my hands moving without my permission? I read over the typed words on the screen. "To meet someone, with the possibility of sex."

"Umm, guess that'll do." The words linger in the air, loaded with hesitation, but I proceed anyway. The next registration step asks me to select the traits and characteristics that best describe myself; friendly, outgoing, extrovert, high-strung, adventurous. The bottom half asks what traits and characteristics I am seeking; friendly, outgoing, free-spirited, adventurous.

This is starting to feel like homework! If I weren't two steps away from completion, I would close my laptop. The next step asks for personal sexual interests and to select up to five men who I find the most physically attractive. "Finally! Thought they would've asked this first." Excitedly clicking the boxes to best describe my preferences: male, no preference of race, heterosexual, dominant, passionate, communicator.

"Oh, my goodness, damn he fine! He fine too!" I scroll the page, gawking at how attractive the men in the photos are. Nearly ten minutes later, I enter my payment information and click the submit button.

"Congratulations! A customer rep will contact you within 24 hours to confirm your membership." I close my laptop and grab my glass of wine. What in the hell did I just do?

Pay to Play - Ch. 3

C laire, the new intern, peeks into my office. "Ms. Brooks, your two o'clock just called to cancel. They rescheduled for next Thursday at three. Is that okay?"

"Yes, that's fine. Did the mailroom deliver those court proceedings from storage yet?"

"No, not yet. I'll call to check the status," Claire replies.

"Thank you. Let me know when they arrive." Claire retreats from my office, closing the door behind her. Thankful for the cancelation; it frees up time to take a longer lunch this afternoon. There's a new deli around the corner that usually has a long wait. Everyone in the office has raved about it for weeks. I may finally be able to try it, plus I should have enough time to shop for Jen's birthday.

I press the intercom button. "Claire, please hold my calls until I return. I'll be back before the Grothwell conference call at 3:30." I grab my coat and purse on the way out of the office.

The automatic lobby doors open. The cool, fresh Chicago air kisses my face. The bright sun illuminates the dullness of the gray city buildings. A smile covers my face, thankful for some freedom away from my stuffy office. Just when I take a deep breath, letting the autumn breeze tousle my curls, my phone buzzes loudly. My heart jumps. I stop to scramble in my purse to locate it before the caller disconnects. "Hello, this is Cincy."

A formal voice greets me on the other end. "Hello, Ms. Brooks?"

"Yes?"

"Hello, my name is Gracie. I'm calling from One for All. Do you have a few moments to speak?"

"Sure, I was just heading out for lunch." Instantly, my nerves cause my hands to shake. My schedule has been so busy today that I completely forgot I registered for an escort service last night.

Gracie's high-pitched tone exclaims, "Oh great! This shouldn't take more than five minutes of your time. Ms. Brooks—"

"Please, call me Cincy."

"My apologies. Cincy, I've been assigned your account. I'm here to personally assist you. I wanted to discuss a few more particulars with you before we continue. Afterwards, I'll send you the contract documents. First, we wanted to know more about you and what you expect from One for All. I want to do all I can to ensure this is a fun and pleasurable experience for you."

My walking pace slows and my legs become weak from nervousness. I decide to sit on a bench near the central fountain and respond, "Thank you for assisting. Well, I'm recently divorced. The dating scene is quite foreign to me now. I hoped this route would serve me better than the usual dating sites."

"I see. That's a great plan. Most people choose us because we specialize in creating discreet dating experiences. Cincy, your profile looks really good. From the pictures you chose, you don't seem to have a particular type in appearance. That could serve you well and simplify my job." Gracie chuckles. "Are there any kinks or fetishes to disclose in your profile?"

I consider how to respond to such an awkward question. "No, no kinks or fetishes. I have a question for you. Is sex negotiable?" My eyes gaze around me to see if anyone overheard my response.

"Oh, of course we are an escort service, but that doesn't mean you or your date is required to have sex. Some clients use escort services for just companionship, dates to corporate events, and other celebrations. The terms clearly state sex is not required in the consent forms. I will send you copies to review and provide your electronic signature. After that, you will be allowed to browse the dating pool. Once you've selected a few people you would like to see, I will review the compatibility and send you an invitation to meet. At least for the first two dates or whenever you are comfortable to schedule on your own. How does that sound?"

Slightly overwhelmed, I reply. "Sounds good to me. I'll look for the forms and contract. Is there anything else I need to know?"

"Cincy, you will have a great time if you open yourself to the experience. Remember this is all about you," she stresses. "It has been a pleasure speaking with you. I'll include my contact information with the forms. I'll be in touch. Have a great day."

"Thank you. You as well."

Pay to Play – Ch. 4

"Tonight, is the night." The infamous song from Betty Wright blasts throughout the bar. Jen and I decided to meet for drinks before my first rendezvous with the hired "help." Gracie, the One for All consultant, guided me through scheduling my first escort. Heeding her advice, I booked a room at a nice hotel downtown. It was Jen's idea to meet at the hotel for drinks before he arrives.

"Girl, my momma used to play this song all the time," Jen says, swaying her body to the beat. "They should have a dance floor in here cause I'm loose as hell right now! This gotta be my last drink cause BJ will flip if he has to come pick me up."

The modern hotel bar has low lighting and a relaxing vibe. The burgundy, gold and black décor is sexy. The way Jen is bouncing in her seat, you would think it was a nightclub.

"Yes, this is the jam. Don't it make you want to two-step or something?" I snicker at our grown folk conversation. "He's supposed to meet me here in like thirty minutes. You still staying until he gets here? Just to make sure it's all good, please."

"Yeah. You nervous at all?"

I nod my head. "Hell yes! I ain't never done anything like this before."

Jen tilts her head. "Awh, you'll be fine. Just take him to the room, fuck him, and go home."

"That simple, huh?"

"Yep. Don't sit here and act like you didn't have a one-night stand before. We did some crazy shit back in college."

I shake my head. Her truth is comforting. "So true."

I observe the room, enjoying the vibe and music. The bar is filled with older men in business suits, except for one man sitting alone in a booth. He's much younger with a low buzz haircut. His brown leather jacket and white t-shirt give him a bad boy look. "Jen. Jen!" I yell over the music. I lean in to tell her, "I think that's the guy over there in the leather jacket."

In her true dramatic fashion, she turns to look over both shoulders. "Who? Where at? Oh, I see. He's cute CiCi." Her eyes widen. "Girl, he getting up."

"I see that. I think he's coming over here." I watch him stroll across the room with a motorcycle helmet in his hand. "Be cool Jen."

She rolls her eyes at me. "No, you be cool!"

He approaches the table. "Hello ladies. How are you doing?" That's definitely the man from the website. Seeing him up-close confirms what I remember from the pictures.

Jen introduces us both. "Hi to you. I'm Jennisha. This is my friend CiCi."

I extend my hand. "Are you Landen?"

He smiles and shakes my hand. "Yes. Cincy? It's nice to meet you."

Jennisha's eyebrows raise in surprise. She reaches for her purse and stands from her seat. "Umm. C, I'm going to go. Are you okay?" Jen says, interrupting our moment.

I nod to her. "Yes, let me know you made it home. I'll call you tomorrow. Night girl."

"Night." She leans in for a quick hug.

I turn my attention back to Landen. "Would you like to sit?"

"We can get out of here if you're ready." He looks deep into my eyes, seeking an answer.

"May I finish my drink first? To be honest, I'm a little nervous."

"My apologies. Not rushing you. Let me take care of the tab while you finish." A relaxed smile covers his face.

I thank him and take another sip of my drink. "You look different from your pictures. You cut off your curly red hair."

His hand brushes the top of his head. "I wanted to do something different. Guessing you liked the ginger afro better?"

I giggle at him making fun of himself. "Actually, I did. I thought it was cute. This looks good on you too, though." I lift my glass, drinking the remainder of my Cosmopolitan. "Think I'm ready now."

He helps me from my seat. "Let's get out of here."

Pay to Play - Ch. 5

Date #1

The Unexpected

Landen L.
Male, White, 6'1"
Hobbies: Gaming, Hiking, Dancing, Cooking, Reading
Sexual Interests: Fun, Spontaneous, Passionate
Kinks: BDSM, Food-play, Role-play, Orgy

Landen holds the elevator door for me. We exit on the 10th floor, heading to the hotel room I booked for the night. The short walk to the room is silent. It's not an awkward or unnerving silence, more so anticipation.

I remove the keycard to unlock the door. Landen breaks the silence. "Let me." He says, gently removing the key from my hand. He swipes the keycard and opens the door for me to enter. The fear of what happens when we get in this room causes my bones to shake. He follows me inside, placing the keycard on the desk.

"Tell me Cincy, what are your expectations for tonight?"

His question was unexpected and caught me completely off guard. I quickly turn to face him. He looks at me over the hood of his eyes with folded arms.

"I'm not exactly sure. Good sex?" Even to myself, the answer sounds uninspiring and boring. "I mean. I don't really know what you're asking."

He removes his jacket and places it over the chair. "I want to know what you want me to do to you. What do you like? I want to give you what you want. That's why I am here, right?"

Exhaling a deep breath, I contemplate his direct words. Yes, I hired him to make me feel good, but didn't consider what that would entail. In my mind, I thought we would just miraculously have sex and not say a word. I'm normally a talkative, inquisitive person, yet for some reason, I didn't account for the verbal communication needed tonight. After a few moments of silence, I respond, "I'm not sure. No one has ever asked me that question."

Landen walks over to me. His hands gently rubbing my arms. "How about we go with the flow. If you decide to meet with me again, maybe that's something you should think about. If you want more or less, something new altogether just say it."

My voice is barely above a whisper; the simplest response escapes my lips. "Okay." My sexual experience probably seems mild compared to the women he's dealt with. Landen, sensing my apprehension, presses his body against mine. He carefully rubs the small of my back. His hard body against mine awakens the feminine parts I've left abandon for far too long. I follow his lead by placing my right hand on his shoulder, rubbing down to his large biceps. There's no doubt he visits the gym regularly to keep his body in shape. Grateful for his dedication, I melt into him. He wraps his large arms around me and kisses me, all in one swift movement. His tongue tastes like bourbon and sweet mint. His manly pheromones mixed with the scent of soap and shampoo invade my senses.

We sloppily kiss, igniting the heated moment between us. It feels like minutes pass before we come up for air. I can't recall the last time I've made out. Maybe my wedding night? We hastily begin stripping off each other's clothes. Landen pulls my body against his again and nibbles on my earlobe before forcibly turning me around. His hard dick pressed against my ass nearly gives me an instant orgasm. Landen walks me over to the floor-to-ceiling windows. The time separated from Savion has done damage to my self-control.

"Ooh Cincy! You look so good." Landen whispers.

My naked body presses against the cold window glass. The

city buildings stare back at me, but I don't care. Engulfed in the moment, I hear the echoes of my moans throughout the room. He cups my breasts in his hands and massages them softly. He then squeezes each dark nipple until they harden.

I reach my hands behind me needing to feel his dick in my hand. So much for white guys having small dicks. The size doesn't resemble what I imagined, especially in relation to a previous experience. It could be considered medium size in my lineup, falling in the four-to-five-inch range. It's the thickness that makes my mouth water. Unable to control the craving, I turn to face him and drop to my knees. I immediately place him in my mouth.

"Fuck yeah," he grunts and places his hand on the window to steady himself.

With hunger, I grab his ass and push him further into my mouth. His length allows me to take all of him with ease. Before I can display my many talents, he reaches down and grabs a handful of my natural, curly hair. Without hesitating, I quickly remove his dick from my mouth. With a stern glare, I say, "No. Don't do that. Don't touch my hair."

"I'm so sorry. Really. Please, I didn't mean to."

"Just don't do it again."

He pulls me to my feet. He says, "Promise."

Sucking his dick is still on my mind, yet I don't want to press it. I assumed I wasn't the first black woman he's been with. The cultural education will wait for now. He only gets one more chance to not fuck this up.

"One sec." Landen pulls away to retrieve a condom from his jeans, opening it and rolling it over his erection. He approaches me and holds me close, pressing my back against the glass. The wet kisses on my neck relieve the unwarranted tension from the previous moments. I invite him inside by lifting my leg and guiding him into my wetness. Finally feeling a dick inside of me is worth the wait. With no more time for formalities, "Fuck me," I demand.

He steadies himself between my thighs. His strokes are short and hard. I couldn't help but look to view him inside me. His pale skin between my dark brown legs is comparable to an ice cream sandwich. It's definitely sweet enough to satisfy my overdue craving.

Yet, I don't want sweet right now. I grab Landen's chin and request, "Turn me around. Landen, fuck me!" He does exactly that. He turns me around and shoves me roughly against the window. He guides himself inside my walls and fucks me so hard my skin squeaks against the glass.

"Yes! Fuck me!"

His hand smacks my ass so hard, tears well in my eyes. He asserts himself by slamming his dick inside me repeatedly over and over. "This what you want."

Landen abruptly pulls his dick out. "What are you doing?" I question his sudden change in behavior. He sits down in the decorative reading chair adjacent to the window. Landen motions for me to sit in his lap.

As I near him, he gently pulls me down into his lap. With my back to him, I rise slightly to guide his dick inside me. Aiming to remember all that was lost, I roll my hips back and forth, up, then down to find a rhythm to match his thrusts. My body desperately seeks an orgasm. I lick my fingers, wetting them enough to coat my clitoris. I rub my clit while riding his dick. The overwhelming feeling to cum overtakes my ability to slow down. "Yes! Yes!" I bounce harder and faster until my walls contract around him. The orgasmic release is swift and fleeting. I lean back against him satisfied with what I could get.

"Fuck yeah," he whispers in my ear while my head rests upon his shoulder.

"I'm sorry. I need to get my leg strength back. I may need a minute."

Landen taps my thigh to stand. "I got you. Come here." He stands and takes my hand, guiding me over to the bed. I lie down seeking to rest my legs. He wastes no time yanking me to the edge of the bed. He slowly enters my pussy, intently watching every stroke. What is he thinking? I consider asking him but refuse to interrupt the vibe with meaningless questions. He's probably taking mental pictures. That look is all too familiar from the days Savion and I started having sex.

"You are so fucking hot," Landen says. He aggressively lifts my legs and hangs them over his shoulders with my ass slightly lifted off the bed. He fucks me so hard that my thighs jiggle. My breasts bounce with each pump. To witness it myself, I prop up on my elbows, taking a few mental pictures of my own to remember this night.

He grunts and cries out, "Scratch me. Come on, Cincy."

"Huh?" Did he just ask me to scratch him?

Landen repeats, "Fucking scratch me!" Astonished by his request, I hesitantly reach for the closest piece of skin and lightly dig my nails into his forearm. "Harder dammit."

This time I dig deeper into his skin, scraping my nails along his arm. My eyes widen with disbelief written on my face. He seems to like it, even as he winces in pain. "Harder. Come on. Make me fucking cum."

I tightly grip his arm, scraping my nails as hard as I can in one long, deep stroke down his arm. He yelps in pain, my body jolts startled from his scream. Blood oozes from the open wounds. "Ah, fuck. Ah, yeah." His grunts loudly ricochet off the walls from his intense orgasm. I watch him stumble backwards to the chair we previously occupied.

I ask, concerned, "Are you okay? Your arm looks painful."

Blood runs down his arm. He sluggishly glances down at the open wound. "It's just a little blood. I'll clean it up. Give me a sec."

"That was new for me. Does the pain like, intensify your orgasm or something like that?"

He looks annoyed by my questions. "Something like that. It kind of sends me over the edge, you know?" Landen abruptly stands and walks to the bathroom to clean up.

Patiently, waiting for him to finish handling his business, I sit up on the edge of the bed. The night has been fun, but I'm ready to get home. My bed is calling my name.

The toilet flushes, water runs in the sink, and the door finally opens. He smiles at me before gathering his clothes from the floor. He dresses quietly. I grab the sheet to cover up suddenly feeling an awkwardness fill the space.

I break the silence. "Thank you. You know, for tonight."

"Same here. Thank you for hiring me. Maybe we could do this again." Landen says, pulling his shirt over his head.

I stand to walk him to the room door. "I'll definitely consider that. Thank you."

He grabs his leather jacket, stopping to kiss me on the cheek on his way out of the door.

Pay to Play - Ch. 6

"Who is calling so early on a Saturday? My cell phone rings continuously. The vibration against the nightstand begins to annoy me." I reach for my phone to glare at the screen, swiping right to accept the call. "Jen, why are you calling so early? Now you know it's been a long week."

"Hey to you too. Excuse me. I thought you'd be up by now. Ugh, don't be so damn snappy."

"Girl, I was trying to rest from this hectic workweek. I'm up now though. Thanks to you."

"Anyways, I was calling to hear about your night with the white boy the other day. How was it?"

It slipped my mind to call her and give the details of the date with Landen. "It was good. I didn't expect his dick to be good, but I was wrong. I dated this guy Payton in high school. The sex was so bad I gave up on white guys. So, I'm really surprised he could fuck. But you know, there was just something missing. I don't know. A disconnect or something. It was nice to be fucked though, especially since the divorce."

"Well, at least you finally got some much-needed dick. You don't have to hire him again. Just have fun. Don't you have a date today, right? What's his name again?" Jen's voice is filled with excitement. You would think she was coming along with me.

Exasperated with her early morning enthusiasm, "His name is Trace, nosy." I put the phone on speaker to lie back down on the pillow. "We're supposed to meet up this afternoon. Kind of weird he preferred the daytime. Crazy right?"

Jennisha's voice raises an octave. "Ooh girl, he probably a superfreak or something. Freaks come out at night, but super-freaks come out after lunch!"

We share an extended laugh.

I end our conversation in order to begin my day. "You are so crazy! Jen, I'll call you later and tell you about it. Cool?"

"Whatever. You better call me later. Forget about me again and see what happen! Bye girl."

The clock reads 8:56 a.m. I reluctantly drag myself out of bed to prepare for the date with Trace.

Pay to Play - Ch. 7

Date #2

The Gentle Giant

Trace B.
Male, Black, 6'5"
Hobbies: Sports, cars, photography, traveling, movies
Sexual Interests: Passionate, Adventurous
Kinks: Bondage, water, fire, tantric

The coffee shop is quiet, excluding the espresso machine and the clinking of glass. There aren't many patrons inside, making it was easy to spot Trace in the far corner by the window.

His eyes are on me as I approach the table. "Trace?"

He stands, "Cincy?"

"Yes. Nice to meet you." We exchange a brief, friendly hug. His height is on full display. Damn black men so fine. I find it difficult to keep my eyes off him. My eyes graze up and down his body. His golden-brown skin, thick eyelashes, defined full lips present much more handsome than his photos.

"Nice to meet you too. You are very beautiful, by the way." The subtle movements of his mouth grasp my attention. I imagine his mouth planting kisses on my body. I thank him for the compliment.

Trace pulls out my chair and asks what I would like to drink. He heads to the front counter to place our order. I wonder if he noticed me checking him out. He glances back and smiles, showing off a sexy dimple in his right cheek.

He returns with a coffee for himself and an herbal tea for me. "Here you go."

"Thank you. I have to ask. How is it you got into this profession?"

"Wow!" The direct question obviously has taken him by surprise. "Going straight into it are we?" He clears his throat. "To be honest, this is my first *job*." He uses his fingers to imitate quotation marks. "I'm new to the city and I don't do well with meeting women. A couple months ago, after a weekly meeting at the firm I overheard some of those crazy, big-shot execs talking about some website called One for All. One day, I was staring at some renderings, lost in thought. Let's just say I was curious enough to check out the website. After considering it for a long while... Well, here I am."

"Why do you have a hard time meeting women? That just seems hard to believe."

"Hmm, good question. I'm still trying to figure that out." A sly smile covers his face.

He's charming, good looking, accomplished. I don't understand how he's a hard time with women. I ponder if he's being genuine or telling me what he thinks I want to hear. "You seem like an interesting guy."

Trace replies, "It's hard being a good guy. Women seem to assume the worst about me, because of how I look, or once they get to know me they try to take advantage of my willingness to please. They assume I'm a fuck-boy or something. Either way, it's only gotten harder the more successful I get in my career." He shrugs his shoulders. "Come on now, that's enough about me. What made you choose me?"

So many questions to his response run through my head. I couldn't shake his explanation of why he volunteered to be an escort. "Hold on. What do you do exactly?"

He says, "I'm an architect.

"So, you don't do this for the money?"

"You ask a lot of questions Cincy. No, I don't. Now, answer my question. Why did you choose me?"

My head lowers with a half-full mug of green tea staring back at me. The answer to his question is loaded one and he probably doesn't want to hear the full backstory of my divorce. I simply reply, "You're very handsome, plus your profile said you have a kink of water. I'm curious."

He stares intently into my eyes. Everything changed in a single moment. I immediately notice the rays of sunlight illuminate his cherrywood colored eyes. His skin is smooth and shiny, like a delicate macaron. I imagine he tastes like salted caramel. We find ourselves engrossed in each other like we discovered a piece of time reserved for only us two. Somehow, the entire room disappears, and I see only him.

His voice reaches a deep-toned whisper. "Ready to go?"

Willingly, I nod yes, nearly pleading to leave this place. We stand from the table. He removes his wallet from his back pocket and leaves a twenty-dollar tip on the table.

Pay to Play – Ch. 8

We enter his modern and spacious condo. Trace closes the door behind us. The living area is mildly decorated but clean. I wouldn't be surprised if he hires a weekly cleaning service to keep his space tidy. Large glass sliding doors cover the wall opposite of the front door. The expansive view of the city is amazing.

"May I kiss you, Cincy?"

I turn to face him, "Now look who's straight to the point!"

"Touché!"

I walk into the living area and place my purse down on his large black sofa. "To answer your question. Yes, you may kiss me." He wastes no time pulling me into his body, leaning down to offer me his beautiful lips. Politely, I oblige by meeting him halfway. He kisses my mouth, my neck, back to my mouth again. Our hands gaining familiarity with the unexplored and unknown. My hands roam up the sleeves of his shirt feeling his smooth skin. The temperature between us quickly heats up as we explore our different erogenous zones.

Trace is the first to break the kiss. "Come on." He grabs my hand and he leads me down a hallway.

At the end of the hallway, bright sunlight pierces through the doorway of a room on the right. We enter his bedroom where a huge king size bed fills the majority of the space. The feathery bed linens and fluffy pillows are white and grey to match the rug and drapes. The slider patio doors provide a similar city and lake view as the living room.

Trace walks away, entering his closet, leaving me standing at the foot of the bed. He quickly returns with a folded t-shirt in hand. He extends the shirt to me.

"Here, put this on." I look around the room, seeking clarification like it would appear out of thin air. Unsure of what or why, I obediently abide by his house rules. My curiosity to know more about him overcomes the uneasiness of stripping naked in front of a man I just met. I slowly begin removing my sundress. The straps fall over my shoulders, permitting the top to fall to my waist. Luckily, the dress didn't require a bra, meaning there was one less piece of clothing to remove. He stares at my bare breasts and they stare back at him. I slip off my wedged heels and pull the dress down over my hips.

"These too?" I ask with my thumbs hooked in my pink thong panty.

He nods slowly. At his request, I pull the panties down to my ankles before reaching out for the t-shirt he still holds. The shirt has to be a large 1x or bigger. Once I let the shirt fall over my body, it swallows me whole. "This is huge, Trace?"

He approaches me and kisses me passionately. "Don't worry. You're still beautiful." His large, thick hands roam my body. A moan escapes my lips when he aggressively grips my ass, damn near lifting me from the ground. On my toes, I reach up to rest my arms around his neck. Trace lifts me in his arms. I wrap my legs around his narrow waist. His strong body feels amazing. I imagine his dick is a true resemblance of its possessor.

We continue with passionate kisses while he carries me into his master bathroom. He settles my feet on the floor and asks, "Let me know if you feel uncomfortable, okay?"

"Okay," I reply, even though I'm unsure where it will lead. He approaches the large glass walk-in shower and turns on the rainfall setting. Does he think he's about to urinate on me? I suddenly feel like I'm playing a role in one of his unexplored fantasies. My heart is racing, and my palms are sweating. Unable to hold my tongue, "Umm, what are you doing?"

"Come over here. I want you to get in."

"Huh? What do you mean? Is urination involved in this anywhere? Because I'm not with that." Should I mention I'd taken a shower before we meet at the café? Not to mention, I just washed and styled my hair last night for this date. Ruining my twist out is not my idea of a good date.

His eyebrows furrow. He scoffs to disguise a light chuckle. "No, no urination!" He seems unbothered by my accusation. "I just want to see you wet. See the water run down your face, your body. Is that too much for you?"

How this gets him off evades me. Even though I don't quite understand, this moment may only happen once. "That's all?" I pout at the thought of messing up my hair. I wouldn't even let Landen touch my hair, yet here I am. To hell with it! I shrug my shoulders and step inside underneath the rainfall. The water falls over my face, ruining my styled hair. My natural curls now soaked down my back. I wipe the water from my eyes in search of Trace. He's quietly leaning against the double sinks located opposite the large shower. The way he wants me turns me on. His lustful gaze roaming over my body causes my pussy to contract. My eyes catch a glimpse of my reflection in the vanity mirror behind him. The white shirt is now translucent and sticking to my brown skin. My full breasts on full display. The dark brown areolas stare back at me.

Trace removes his shirt and tosses it to the floor. Next, he unbuttons his pants. I prepare for him to continue this little strip tease and join me. Instead, he licks his lips and reaches his right hand into his pants. He begins stroking himself. I watch in anticipation to finally see the dick my mind has wondered about since first seeing his pictures. He watches me like the live porn I am. To contribute, I step underneath the water, turning around for him to see my round, desirable ass. I arch my back under the water for his amusement.

A cool breeze creeps across my legs. I wipe the water from my eyes. Trace's hand touches my arm, startling me. I look to find him standing behind me, completely naked. My eyes dropping down to see the dick I've waited all day to see. "Hi there," I say to him and his dick. My hand reach to touch it. It's so large that it spills out of my small hands.

The woodsy cologne scent exuding from him intoxicates me. He leans down to kiss me. My tongue explores his mouth. The shower has turned steamy. The glass is now frosted from either the warmth of the water or the fire we've started. Trace kneels in front of me, lifting the oversized shirt and burying his face between my thighs.

"Oh my god!" I yelp.

My walls contract from the noises of Trace slurping water off my pussy. He sucks on my clit, nearly pulling the soul from my body. The slight pain of him sucking and nibbling on my clit makes my pussy throb. "Umm. That feels so good!" The moans freely escape me. He flicks his tongue against my clit. He slurps. He sucks. He repeats again and again.

My eyes fall upon the vanity mirror again. The image of him kneeling, along with him expertly eating my pussy, sends ripples through me. I moan his name. "Trace! Right there."

The tingling in my pussy signifies my release is near. He grips my ass and applies pressure with every stroke of his tongue. The orgasm slowly creeps up my body and overcomes me so intensely that I buck wildly with every contraction of my walls.

Trace holds me tight against him after my knees slightly buckle. Never letting me go, he stands and turns off the water. A content smile spreads across my face. The orgasm wiped away any stress or anxiety carried into this day. He looks into my eyes and he helps removes the wet shirt from my body, leaving it on the shower floor.

His strong hands guide me back to his bedroom. I immediately collapse on his large, comfy bed. He says, "Wait here." I can't help but stare at his tight ass and long legs exiting the bedroom.

My thoughts linger on how this incredible day began. A cup of tea one minute and an orgasm the next. I turn on to my side and peer out at the city view. The sky is clear and sunny. It's so quiet.

I feel a hand massaging my right thigh. My body jolts, the embarrassment is written all over my face. "Was I asleep?"

"Yeah, I think you dozed off. I was only gone a couple of minutes." Trace laughs. "You good?"

"I'm so sorry! Your bed shouldn't feel so good."

"Here's some water." He hands me the glass. I take a few sips and extend the glass back to him.

"No, drink more. I need you hydrated, beautiful."

"Umm, okay?" Feeling no need to question him, I drink nearly half of the glass.

I'm beginning to notice unpredictable layers to his good-guy persona. He's probably the nice guy until he's fucking the shit out of you all night. Or possibly he's exceedingly kind until you push his buttons. It's astonishing how safe I feel, yet also unsure of who this man is?

Trace removes the glass from my hand, placing it on the nightstand before leaning in to kiss me. His sexual aura easily pulls me into his universe. Unable to control myself, I gently suck on his bottom lip. He positions himself on top of me, easing my back onto the pillows. Trace nestles in the comfortable space between my thighs. His bare erection rubs against my vagina. With all my strength, I roll him over on his back. He's shocked by my sudden move. "Okay, look at you!"

"You have a really big dick."

"Do I now?" He says it as a statement more than a question. He reaches to open the nightstand drawer, removing two condoms.

"Yes, you do."

I slowly crawl down his body to taste him. His dick is delicious. "Shit!" he exclaims.

I open wide and focus my attention on the sensitive tip that fits perfectly snug against my tongue. I stroke him with my hand and moan deeply. I'm enjoying the close-up view. I remove his dick from my mouth and stare its glory, taking a mental pic for later. His dick throbs against my hand. I spit on the tip and spread it down his shaft with my tongue. I take the head into my mouth again and apply pressure with my lips.

Trace interrupts my concentration, tapping me on the shoulder. "Damn, what you trying to do to me? Come here." I seductively crawl up his body. He opens a condom and sheaths himself. Now straddling him, I lift my body to guide his dick inside of me. The girth of him stretches me wide. The pain slowly subsiding with each stroke. I slowly rock my hips back and forth.

"I can't take it all! Fuck, I can't."

The words flow without thought. I find myself completely lost in the satisfying feel of him inside me. My hands grip my breasts and massage my hard nipples. My hips pick up speed, grinding faster and faster. Trace pulls me down for a kiss. Our skin touches in the most intimate way. He instantly devours my mouth with rough, firm kisses. His sexual language has to be passionate touch. The way he uses his hands, match perfectly to my need for affirmation.

His hands travel from my ass to my thighs while I grind my hips. A lax moan flows from his lips.

"Turn over." Trace's low baritone voice vibrates through my body. He flips me over onto my back with his body positioned between my thighs again. The look on his face is either frustration, anger, or concentration. Concerned, I ask, "Everything okay?"

He chuckles. "Yeah. Why, you alright?"

"Perfect!" I ease him inside me. The strokes are slow and melodic. My hips rock to meet his midway, but Trace stops again. Before the question leaves my lips, he closes my thighs and pins them to my chest. He slowly long strokes me, digging deeper with each stroke.

"Oh my god!" The deeper he drills in my pussy, the harder he strokes. His dick touches unknown places, and his aggressiveness is causing me to lose control of my bladder. "Trace. I think I need to use the bathroom."

He strokes faster, ignoring my pleas. "Hold it," he says.

"Trace!" I whimper, feeling involuntary fluids leaking from my body with each continued stroke. The squishing sound of liquid grows louder. "Trace, please!"

Trace pulls out quickly, prompting my pussy to squirt fluid on him and his bed. My eyes grow wide with surprise. This has never happened before. I've seen in it performed in porn before, but never attempted to achieve it for myself. Not to mention, Savion was a prude and would never do anything Trace has done to me today.

Trace re-enters me, repeating the fast hard strokes, encouraging me to squirt again. I wonder what woman showed him these moves. I will forever be grateful for her. Trace doesn't stop there. He goes in for more, riding me wildly with no reserve. I wrap my legs around his waist to pull him closer. I grip his ass and pull him deeper. "Cincy! Cincy!" He cries out my name in orgasm. His large body shudders on top of me.

He rolls over to lie beside me, breathing heavily. I snuggle up to him. He places a quick peck on my lips.

"That was . . . Wow, I didn't know I could do that."

We both lie physically exhausted yet satisfied. With heavy and labored breathing, he says, "That was sexy." A smile covers my face at the compliment.

"Tell me you have a cleaning service to clean this up?" I giggle. I leisurely rise from the bed, standing to search for my clothes.

He chuckles. "Yeah, I'll handle it. You leaving? I can order some lunch if you want." His voice changes from playful to anxious.

I look into his beautiful brown eyes and study his handsome face. I consider taking him up on his offer, but something warns me to not overstay my welcome. "Maybe some other time. Let's not mess up a good time."

He nods his head up and down, but refused to look at me. He's clearly disappointed, but not willing to fight with me. "It's whatever you want Cincy. Can we keep in touch?"

"For sure. Thank you for the coffee, Trace." I offer a sly smile. "And the dick."

Pay to Play - Ch. 9

The computer screen stares at me. I've been unable to focus on any of my tasks for the day. Trace has been on my mind since our date last week. The recollections are reoccurring in my head on a loop. It's proving problematic to not get him off my mind. I have work and things to do besides thinking about him all day. Yet, the way his body felt against mine. The way he pushed me to new limits. They evade every minute of untenanted mental space.

I stand from my desk and close my office door from prying ears. I grab my cell phone and dial Jennisha's number. Her input could prove useful right now.

Jen picks up on the second ring. "Cici, what's up girl?"

"Hey girl, what you doing?"

She tells me here whereabouts. "Nothing much. About to cater lunch for a supply company on the Eastside. I just need to drop off the food and then I'm done for today. What's up with you?"

My eyes glance over my scheduled appointments for today. "Wanted to see if you could meet for lunch today. I'm free between two and four this afternoon."

"Are you okay? You sound like you need to talk."

"You know me too well. You free or not?"

"Ugh, don't act like that. Yeah, come by my place at two. I'll whip up some lunch."

This is the exact reason I love her. "Thanks girl. See you then."

∞ ∞ ∞

Jennisha answers the door. "Hey girl, come on in!" We embrace in a brief hug. I close the door behind me and follow her to the modern open kitchen located in the rear of the home. Her home is beautiful with a kitchen top chefs would envy. I sit at the large white marble island, placing my purse on the empty stool beside me.

Jennisha stirs something in a pot. Whatever it is, it smells delicious! "What did you cook?"

"Just a little something. Some chicken and white bean soup, with some sourdough bread."

"That sounds good. You making this for dinner, aren't you?" I give her a smirk. "I thought I was special."

She laughs at the remark. "Yeah, you right. BJ requested it last night. You're welcome to some though." She replaces the lid on the pot. "So, what you need to talk about? You had me worried on the way home."

Sighing heavily, I ramble off my thoughts. "Remember, the guy Trace from the afternoon date last week. Girl, he was so damn fine! For real tall, dark and handsome. I can't stop thinking about him. I can barely get anything done at work. The sex was amazing! My goodness it was crazy good. Honestly, I don't know if that's the main reason I can't stop thinking about him or if I really like him. I promise girl, I think we had this moment at the coffee shop."

Jen interrupts me. "Hold up. What you mean you had a moment?"

"It's hard to explain. It was just different. I never felt it before. Not with Savion or any guy I've met. It was like . . . Like the room went quiet and it was only us there. We were in our own world. It was beautiful. I didn't say anything to him about it. We just went to his place and fucked, then I left."

"I mean, how did he act? What you going to do?" Jennisha asks.

I look at her, "He seemed a little disappointed I was leaving. I just thought it was best to leave since he finished the job, you know. Honestly, I don't know what to do. Do I hire him again? Isn't that weird though? Why couldn't we have just met like normal people like you said. Maybe then I would trust that he was into me too."

"You think because he was paid to spend time with you, that what you felt wasn't real?"

"Exactly. What do I do Jen? If I hire him and ask to see him outside of the escort service, he might think I just don't want to pay him." My hands cover my face in embarrassment.

"Listen Ci, you know what you need to do. Hire him again and see what happens. You may be surprised to find that he likes you too. You never know."

I shake my head hoping the confusion would fall away. "There's more. I hired this guy Erick, scheduled for next week. He seems like the kinky freaky bad boy type. I just wanted to try it out before I close my account with One for All. Now I don't know."

Jen looks at me in shock. "Now you come over here spilling your heart. Then in the same breath you talking about getting turned out. You are too much! I think you should hit the Trace guy up first, before you go on that other date. Don't taint what could be." Jen puts her hands on her hip. She's serious and giving her best adult advice.

"I know. I know. You right. This is too much." I scramble through my purse to locate my phone. Her advice rings some truth I desperately needed to hear. I open the One for All app on my phone and search for Trace, clicking the scheduler option.

"Then don't make it harder than it has to be. What are you doing?" she asks.

"Checking to see if he's available this Saturday." My palms sweat, nervously waiting for the scheduler to return the availability results. A message appears stating no availability. I check again for Friday instead. Again, no availability. "It says he's not available this weekend."

Jennisha notices the sadness on my face. "It'll be okay. Just don't give up."

I check for a weekday early next week. Finally, it displays he's available Tuesday night. "Okay, I just scheduled for Tuesday night. Of course, it has to be the night before I meet with the Erick guy," I say rolling my eyes and throwing my hands up in the air.

"Well, that's better than nothing. Cici, give it try. If it works cancel the other guy."

Feeling slightly relieved with clarification of the situation, "That's why you my friend! Now give me some of that soup. I'm starving over here."

Pay to Play - Ch. 10

The hotel lobby is packed with a large group of tourists. The cameras hanging around their necks and the walking shoes are a dead giveaway. Patiently, I wait for Trace to walk through those automatic doors. For the third time in less than five minutes, I check my phone for a notification. We're scheduled to meet in ten minutes. I glance up to find Trace walking towards me. A smile instantly covers my face. He's as good looking as I remembered. His long legs stride confidently through the crowded lobby. "Hello there."

He leans down to hug me. "Hello to you. How are you?"

His disposition is undetectable. The hug was quick but the look in his eyes is seductive. "I'm well. Looking forward to seeing you. Did you want to get a drink, or would you like to go up to the room?"

Trace peers down at me. "Let's head up." Still, I cannot decipher if he means that in a 'this a business' tone or 'I want to fuck you' tone. I grab my purse and phone from the table. His hand is on the small of my back. We head towards the elevator and take the short ride up to the seventh-floor, conversing in small talk.

"Here we are." With the keycard in hand, I open the door to the room. Immediately upon entering the room, I turn around to look directly into Trace's eyes, hoping they would guide me to his soul.

Trace reciprocates the eye contact. He wastes no time taking me into his arms. He says, "I assume you enjoyed yourself last time. You came back from seconds?"

I giggle like a schoolgirl. "I, umm. . . I had a great time with you. I really wanted to talk to you if that's okay? I mean, I want to more than talk, but you get what I mean."

He chuckles nervously. "Okay Cincy, what is it you want to talk about?" He leans back against the entry wall, folding his arms over his chest. His guarded body language nearly deters me from relaying my thoughts.

"Again, I had such a great time with you. I thought there may have been something more. I don't know if that was just me or if you felt it too. So, I wanted to know your thoughts."

He clears his throat. "Look, beautiful. I tried to spend more time with you. You left me lying there. I thought you didn't feel me like that. I wasn't going to press you, especially when you had all the control. I was feeling you the moment you walked into the coffee shop. I knew you were different."

I recall when he asked to get lunch after we fucked. "Yeah, I ran. I didn't know what I was feeling or how to handle the situation in the moment. I admit I was wrong . . . and I would like to see you outside of One for All."

His head lowers, exhaling a long breath. He slowly raises his eyes to meet mine. "I like you, Cincy. I wanna see you more, but you need to understand that I'm a single man until I'm not. Are you okay with that?

"Are you saying you will continue working for One for All?"

"What I'm saying is that, if this goes somewhere," he points his finger back and forth between us, "I'll drop it all."

I ponder his statement. "I guess I understand where you coming from. I don't care to entertain anyone else but you. But since we're keeping options open I notion that. On that note, there is one more thing. I'm scheduled with a guy later this week that I'm not sure about anymore. Since meeting you and all. Honestly, I wanted to meet with you beforehand. You know, to see if I should cancel." I don't know why I mentioned that to him. Maybe his honesty rubbed off.

He asks, "Why did you schedule a date with him Cincy?"

Not sure if I should give him the real reason. All I could manage to say is, "Umm, he seemed really kinky and dominating."

He offers no response, but after a moment of silence, Trace closes the space between us. His height towering over me, prompting me to look up at him.

"Kinky, huh?" He says, lifting his hands to massage my breasts. "Dominating, huh?"

Trace guides his left hand from my breast up to my neck, lightly choking me. My breathing grows ragged. His dominant behavior takes me by surprise. "You like that don't you?" His hands continue to roam upward through my pressed hair. He yanks it so hard I gasp for air.

He says, "Answer me."

"Yes, I like it." I lean in to kiss his soft lips. His strong tongue enters my mouth, the kiss is hard and passionate. "I want you to take me. Please fuck me," I beg. Unbuttoning his shirt to reveal his delicious brown skin, I mimic him by removing my crop top. I step out of my heels. Just as I begin to unbutton my jeans, Trace yanks me by the top of my jeans and guides me to the bed. He pushes me back on the bed.

"May I take these off?" Enthused by his domineering attitude, I ask for permission to remove my pants.

"No. I'll tell you when. Right now, you're gone suck my dick." The look in his eyes is deviant. The energy in the room is fully charged. I'm thoroughly enjoying this side of him. Keeping my eyes on him, I reach to help him remove his jeans. He removes a pack of condoms from his pocket and places them on the nightstand. In an attempt to match his energy, I lie down with my head hanging off the foot of the bed.

"What are you doing?" he asks.

"Feed me." I open my mouth wide for an exaggerated effect.

Trace silently chuckles. He stands unmoved staring at me, probably anticipating what he could do with a warm wet mouth. He removes his boxer briefs and kneels on the bench at the foot of the bed. He slowly guides his dick in my mouth. I underestimated the exhilaration, yet difficulty, of sucking dick upside down. He feeds me his dick, fucking my face slowly at first. Allowing the wetness to cover his shaft. Gradually, he settles on a stable pace. His dick hitting the back of my throat while his balls slap against my forehead.

Trace removes his dick from my mouth. "Why did—"

"Don't question me. Don't fuck this up."

His demeanor is sincere, yet firm. Obediently, I zip my lips shut. Trace proceeds by lifting himself just enough to lower his balls onto my face. Instinctively, I stick out my tongue to taste him. His manly scent will forever be etched in my mind. When I take his balls into my mouth, he releases a lengthy grunt.

"Take this off." He tugs at my bra. With one hand, I reach behind my back to unsnap the bra. He helps remove the straps from my shoulders, allowing me to return to the task at hand of tickling his balls with my mouth. His hands massage my breasts.

Trace strokes his dick against my breasts, teasing my nipples until they harden under his touch. What feels like saliva falls on my chest. Trace squeezes my breasts together and slides his dick in between. I fondle his gooch and grip his ass. My tongue finding its way to his asshole. He releases another lengthy moan. This time cursing aloud. "Damn!"

His strokes pick up speed, barely allowing time for me to match his beat. I work my tongue wildly in quest of his release. His strokes are fast and wild.

"Fuck Cincy."

He orgasms hard, cumming all over my breasts. I soak in yet another new experience. Trace rolls over and collapses against the bed.

"Damn girl. I swear."

Cautiously, I sit up and make my way to the bathroom, hoping not to spread the mess he left on my chest. After cleaning up, still in my jeans, I return to the bed to lie beside Trace. He opens his arm, making room for me to snuggle against him. "I should probably go ahead and cancel that date, huh?"

He looks at me. "Is that a question?" His words full of sarcasm.

I climb out of the bed to retrieve my phone from my purse.

"Where you going? You doing this again?" he asks.

"Just getting my phone so I can cancel." I unlock my phone and notice the app One for All displays a new message. I open the message from Erick and read the first few sentences. "Oh my gosh!"

Trace asks, "You, okay?"

"Wow, this is so crazy! Umm, that guy sent a message. He invited me to a sex party Thursday night. What the hell?" I look to Trace for some guidance. He says nothing. I've never attended a sex party, but this definitely doesn't seem to be the right time. I open the calendar in the One for All app, clicking the cancel button for the date scheduled with Erick on Wednesday. "I canceled the date."

"Where is this sex party?"

I reply, "It doesn't give a city. There's only a street address."

"Let's go. If you want…"

I look at him in disbelief. "Are you serious? Have you been to one before? I don't know if that's my speed."

He shrugs his shoulders. "Just saying. You never been so why not go? You'll be with me. Ol' dude probably don't care who show up."

Contemplating his argument, he has a point. Granted, I've never met or slept with Erick. "What if it's actually his party though? That's straight savage."

"If you care that much, we don't have to."

"Trace, this is wild." I pace the floor. "The experience would be crazy, but I don't know. Shouldn't I at least message him about coming to the party?"

Frustrated, he leaves the decision in my hands. "It's up to you. Do what you want Cincy."

I stop pacing and stare at his fine ass lying there in his full naked glory. "Let's do it." Filled with excitement, I plop down on the bed beside Trace.

He smiles at me, stroking his dick. "Let's do it, but you gotta do me first though."

Pay to Play - Ch. 11

Date #3
The Kinkiest

Erick S.
Male, Black, 5'10"
Hobbies: Sex, Fashion, Partying with friends
Sexual Interests: Adventurous, Free-spirited, Selfless
Kinks: Domination, Bondage, Role-play, Exhibition, Orgy

The historical neighborhood street is lined with immaculate classic mansions. "This is a beautiful home!" I squeal.

Trace pulls up to the valet at the end of the driveway. It appears to be over ten thousand square feet of living space. "Wow, I can't wait to see the interior!"

The car ride to the outskirts of the city was fairly quiet. He's usually talkative and upbeat, but not tonight. His demeanor is chill and reserved.

The valet attendants open the doors for us to exit the car. Trace takes the numbered ticket and places it in his pocket. He reaches for my hand, and we head up the paved driveway. "You sure you're, okay? A lot on your mind?" I ask.

"Naw, I'm good. This house is crazy big." His eyes darting upward to the large exterior second-story windows.

"You nervous at all? It's both our first time. It's nice to experience this together."

He replies with a deep chuckle. "Excited, nervous, I don't know what I feel right now. You really up for this, baby?"

I give a side-eye glance. "I don't know."

We approach the tall, decorative steel and glass double doors. The host tending the door asks for a name. I provide the attendant with my name, and after a few seconds of him searching his list, he opens the doors. "Please enjoy."

Trace and I share a look with one another before stepping inside. A look denoting more than words could express. Either this will be a fun night of new experiences, or it will end in disaster. The foyer is decorated in classic black and white. The traditional railing on the staircase and classic paintings accentuates the formal Victorian design.

We observe the other partygoers standing around the foyer. Everyone is dressed in white attire. Unfortunately, Trace and I missed that memo. We are both wearing black tonight, easily standing out amongst the crowd. My hand grips Trace's hand tightly. He must have sensed my body language because he guides me to a room located to the right of the entrance. His height must have helped him spot the bar. He wastes no time maneuvering through the crowd.

Trace asks the bartender for two neat bourbons. The room is small, but noisy. The vibe is casual; you would suspect it was a normal gathering. People are conversing and laughing.

"Here you go." Trace hands me a glass of bourbon. The strong brown liquid coats my throat. "Drink up," he says. I laugh internally, understanding fully what he means.

"I might need another," I say. We share a quick laugh at ourselves. It's obvious we're out of place being the rookies that need a buzz to let loose. "Doesn't seem so bad, right?"

He whispers in my ear. "This seems too chill. I don't think we've gotten to the good part yet." I nod my head in agreement. Trace finishes his drink, setting his glass on the counter. He signals to the bartender for another round confirming his nervousness. The liquid courage quickly takes effect on me. I lean against Trace seeking some familiarity. He leans down, placing a few quick kisses on my lips. I finish my drink and give Trace the empty glass. Just as he places it on the counter, the bartender slides over the second round.

Trace hands me the second bourbon. He says, "Come on. Let's go check this place out." He takes my hand, leading us toward the foyer. We finish our drinks while exploring the first floor of the mansion. Most of the rooms are empty. We notice a few people making out in a hallway. We approach a dark hallway to find it leads to a downstairs basement.

I mention to Trace, "That must be where the party is."

Trace leads the way down the stairs into a dimly lit space illuminated by soft white candles. The room is stark white. White walls, white fabric hanging from the ceiling, white sofas, white chairs. Why did we choose to wear all black again? Our attire offers nowhere to hide. A fully naked woman approaches us. Where did she come from?

"This your first time, huh?" She's young, lighter complexion, maybe in her early twenties. She's fully uncovered, holding conversation without any reservation. Her figure is extremely thin. If it weren't for the fake breasts, she would be sticks and bones.

I finally reply, "Yes. We wanted to try something new." Trace is behind me, snuggled tightly against my ass. He may be just as uncomfortable as I, yet his partial erection poking me says otherwise.

"I'm Sugar by the way. I can show you around. Y'all follow me." Sugar grabs my hand, a bit too possessive for my liking, pulling me along with her.

"Where are we going?" I wonder if she heard me over the excessive moaning throughout the room. We pass a woman getting fucked from behind by a fat white man. Next to them, there's a threesome with a woman sucking one man's dick while getting her pussy licked by another man. If Sugar wasn't walking so fast, I could have witnessed more. We approach a room on the opposite side in the far corner. There's no door, just sheer white curtains covering the doorframe.

I squeeze Trace's hand, not knowing where Sugar has led us. Sugar parts the curtains to enter the room. Trace and I follow her inside. A dark-skinned man lays on a white bed with huge white pillows. A blonde-haired woman's ass is tooted in the air, sucking his dick from a side angle, giving us a clear view of their action. Upon closer inspection, the man looks very familiar. "Erick?" I say curiously, not intending to say it aloud.

Erick, the guy I almost hired from One for All, peeks around the head of the blonde-haired woman. "Hey beautiful. What's up?" He gives a seductive smile. He looks just as good as his photos. His glowing white smile and defined muscles make my pussy turn flips. He observes my eyes enthralled on his dick. Erick choosing to show off, grabs the head of the blonde-haired woman, forcing her head down onto his dick. He slaps her ass with his other hand. I turn to face Trace, feeling the need to check in with him. Like the two beginners we are, we continue standing near the doorway. Neither of us have moved since following Sugar into the room.

Seeking some type of non-verbal communication, I lean into him. He looks down into my eyes, then back to the scene unfolding on the bed. I turn around to witness for myself. Sugar has climbed onto the bed and is kissing Erick while rubbing his chest. Erick's hand clinches Sugar's jaw, holding her face steady. Trace's erection is growing harder. Sugar clearly turns him on. He's had a hard-on since seeing her. I move my hand behind my back to feel him up. His hands roam my body, pausing at my breasts. Trace's hand massages my breast; with the other hand, he tilts my head back in search of my mouth. He kisses me with hunger. My legs begin to shake when he pulls up my dress over my ass to reveal my bare pussy. His hand travels to my sweet spot, playing with my clit while he watches the sexual activities unfolding on the bed.

Erick whispers something in Sugar's ear. She rises from the bed and comes over to where Trace and I stand. No warning, no permission. She boldly kisses me and grabs both of my breasts. She unties the halter top of my dress and lustfully watches the fabric fall. She kisses me again and fondles my bare breasts. I stand sandwiched between her and Trace. Trace's dick is twitching against my ass.

Next, Sugar tugs my arm, pulling me over to the bed. I sit, but my eyes are glued on Trace. Sugar drops to her knees and spreads my legs, her face landing in pussy. Her possessiveness is both her strength and weakness. The assertiveness serves her well, yet it feels overly dominant. All my concerns subside when her tongue licks the exact spot Trace's hand just occupied. She opens her mouth wide and slurps. She slurps and sucks. She licks and sucks. A moan falls from my lips. Erick's strong hand rubs my arm. He leans over and roughly massages my breast.

Without warning, Trace grabs my arm and yanks me from the bed. Sugar falls back, nearly landing on her ass. Trace glares at Erick before tugging and practically dragging me from the room. I attempt to pull down my dress, stumbling behind him. He makes a beeline back toward the stairs to exit the basement.

"Trace!" I yell after him.

"We're leaving," he says as we reach the front foyer.

"What happened? Why are you mad?" I yell attempting to keep pace with his long strides. He ignores my questions.

We exit the house. I can't grasp what happened for him to become so angry. What did I do? Trace grabs my hand to follow him to the valet stand. He gives the attendant our ticket to retrieve the car. While we wait, he turns towards me. "Why'd you let him touch you? You broke the rule, Cincy." His voice is stern.

"Excuse you? That's what this is about?" I look upside his head. "No, no, no! You said I couldn't fuck another man. You did not say touch, so no I didn't break the rule. You need to figure out why you're so mad cause this has nothing to do with me. Why would you fuck up the night like this?"

The valet pulls up with the car. Trace opens the passenger door for me before entering the driver's seat. He hands the valet a tip and closes the door. "For real Cincy, seeing him touch you didn't sit right with me. That shit got me angry. I'm being honest with you."

"Wait. So, the girl licking my pussy didn't upset you, but Erick touching me did? Make it make sense Trace."

"You exactly right! You not about to fuck me and think I'm okay with some other dude in your face!"

I reply, "Trace, this was your idea to go. If you don't want to share me then say that. Don't do shit like this and embarrass us both."

"Hell no I don't want to share you. Shit, I just found you. What if you would have gave that nigga head or some shit. He'd be headhunting trying to find your ass. I ain't got time for that shit!"

I chuckle at his comment, not meaning to dismiss his feelings. "Headhunting? What does that mean?"

"Your head so good you make a nigga go out of his way to get at you again. Don't fuck with me Cincy. You know what I'm talking about."

I laugh from my belly. I haven't even given him my best head yet, and he already acting up. "I've never heard that before. You just made that up!"

"It ain't that funny." His anger level decreasing. He laughs in response to watching me laugh.

"I'll take the compliment. But don't act like that again. I'm not responsible for your insecurities. We discussed the boundaries and I kept them. You didn't." I stare at him.

Trace apologizes. "Look, I'm sorry. I get it. Sorry I ruined the night for you."

After a few moments of silence, he looks over at me. He reaches over and squeezes my thigh. "Forgive me?"

He better be glad I like him. Leaning over the middle console, I kiss his neck while he drives. Unbuttoning his slacks, I rub his dick through the lightweight fabric.

"Yes. Now, how long until we get back to your place? Dare you to bet against me." I say while removing his dick from his briefs and placing my head in his lap.

Pay to Play – Ch. 12

Jennisha looks at me over the rim of her glass. A disgusted frown covers her face.

"What?" I ask.

She purses her lips. "You know what! I knew you should've gone on that date with Erick. Damn, I want to know what would've happened now. The way you painted the picture, got me over her like..." She fans herself with her hand.

I shake my head at her comment. "Girl, he would've been too much for me. He's a one-time kind of thing. You right though, it probably would have been an eventful night if we would've let it play out."

"So, you and Trace good though? How you hire an escort and end up finding a man!" She raises her hand for a high-five.

Trace and I are doing very well, yet his episode at the party bothered me for a few days. He was so highly insecure and possessive that I wondered if he would react the same with any man in my presence or if it was just Erick.

After speaking with him, he finally admitted he thought he had one-upped on Erick, which is why he wanted to go to the party. What he didn't admit, and what I believe to be true, is that he realized he wasn't the only alpha male in that room, causing him to act out of character. He was left standing there by himself, watching another man touch his girl. Trace could have just as easily demanded my attention in the moment, yet he chose to act immaturely.

From the unexpected to the fun kinky sex, I have to admit the experience was worthwhile. Now that Trace has quit One for All, I'm excited to see where this goes.

I respond to Jen, "Yeah, we're good. He's a really good guy, Jen. Figured I could pay to play a little bit and somehow Trace happened."

www.ingramcontent.com/pod-product-compliance
Lightning Source LLC
Chambersburg PA
CBHW071616150726
48000CB00004B/1738